W. R. Hill

To May

Thanks and Best

Wishes always —

Rand Hill

March 2015

Text copyright © 2014 W.R. Hill

All Rights Reserved

For my wonderful wife Pat.

Thanks for all your love, support and encouragement through all my crazy endeavors.

Table of Contents

Chapter 1

Chapter 2

Chapter 3

Chapter 4

Chapter 5

Chapter 6

Chapter 7

Chapter 8

Chapter 9

Chapter 10

Chapter 11

Chapter 12

Chapter 13

Chapter 14

Chapter 15

Chapter 16

Chapter 17

Chapter 18

Chapter 19

Chapter 20

Chapter 21

Chapter 22

Chapter 23

Chapter 24

Chapter 25

Chapter 26

Chapter 27

Chapter 28

Chapter 29

Chapter 30

Chapter 31

Chapter 32

Chapter 33

Chapter 34

Chapter 35

Chapter 36

Chapter 37

Chapter 38

Chapter 39

Chapter 40

Chapter 41

Chapter 42

Chapter 43

Chapter 44

Chapter 45

Chapter 46

Chapter 47

Chapter 48

Chapter 49

Chapter 50

Chapter One

Ballinger left his hotel at five that morning dressed in workout sweats, carrying a gym bag stuffed with the disassembled Barret M82A1 sniper rifle, a Glock 17 and a change of clothes. As a Marine sniper in Iraq he killed for love of country. Now he kills for love of money.

The weather was typical for a February in Vienna, very cold in the mornings warming to the mid-forties by afternoon. The sky was overcast and a light fog was creeping in from the Danube. A slight mist hung in the air as he walked down damp empty streets. The street lights shined a pale yellow in the fog. Ballinger pulled the hood up on his sweatshirt to ward off the morning chill. He walked the six blocks to the Zurich building looking like any other gym rat headed to his early morning workout. He had an angular face, stood a little over six feet tall and weighed in at 220. With scant body fat and muscles reinforced by steroids, he could have passed as a wide receiver with the Dallas Cowboys. He looked a lot like that guy Howie what's-his-name, the football sportscaster, only without the fifties flat top haircut.

He stopped next to the building, gave the periphery a quick glance and ducked into the dark alley. The space between the man-made monoliths was filled with molding trash bags, cigarette butts, fast food wrappers and empty cardboard boxes, all crammed against a couple of rusting dumpsters. He pulled on a pair of latex gloves and opened the lid on the dumpster nearest the Zurich building, then, he picked the lock on the delivery door and went inside. In the dim light of the shipping area he disabled the proximity alarm well within the thirty seconds it took to register an intrusion. He stepped into the utility elevator, punched the button for the executive floor and hummed *Margaritaville* to himself on the ride up. When the doors opened, he crossed to enter the stairwell and noted the fire alarm box on the wall, *perfect* he thought to himself. He took the stairs two at a time up one flight. He came to a long hallway with a ladder to the roof attached to the wall at the end. He climbed the ladder, opened the hatch and stepped into the cool crisp air on the roof.

Ballinger stood motionless in the darkness surrounded by the early morning silence. He surveyed the roof. Six HVAC units stood like giant sentries at their posts silently keeping watch over the city. They were painted a dark gray with spots of rust at the corners brought on by harsh wet winters and dry summers. As his eyes adjusted to the dim light, he settled in behind the unit giving the clearest view of the OPEC building's southwest door some 750 yards away. He sat still in the crisp morning darkness visualizing what was to come, acquiring the target, taking the shot, the ensuing chaos and making his exit.

Twelve stories below as the sun crept over the horizon pushing its way through the clouds and morning mist, Vienna came to life. Early morning delivery trucks dropped off goods to shops and cafes.

The smell of fresh breads and other pastries being baked wafted through the streets. Bundles of newspapers hit street corners, to be retrieved by sleep weary vendors and sold in small downtown shops. In a few more hours the city would be a bustling hub of activity.

Ballinger began the rifle assembly. The Barret M82A1weighs just under thirty pounds and is four feet long fully assembled. It shoots a .50 caliber bullet that leaves the barrel traveling 2,799 feet per second. The weapon is accurate up to a distance of just over 1,900 yards. At a cost of $8,900 each, the U.S. Marine Corps bought 125 of them for use in Desert Shield and Desert Storm in Kuwait and Iraq. Your tax dollars at work.

Ballinger grew up the youngest of four brothers, each of whom had a different father. His mother, Louise was an attractive and extremely intelligent woman. She would generally bring home men of lesser intelligence who were easily manipulated. A couple of them actually married her. She used them up, got what she wanted, usually in the form of cash or real estate and sent them packing. There were a few live-in lovers as well who quickly met the same fate.

Louise moved often, always taking the kids with her which meant they'd be out of school for months at a time. Most of the kids' fathers never knew where they were and probably didn't care. Louise never had any real interest in being a parent. She was totally focused on herself. All the boys were pretty much left to raise themselves. As the youngest, Ballinger was often picked on by his older half brothers and by the older kids at the six different schools he went to in his six years of elementary school. When he got to high school he enjoyed a growth spurt that made him one of the biggest kids in the school. He spent a great deal of time in detention, always in trouble, mostly for fighting. He particularly enjoyed going after cheerleader boyfriends. These were the kind of guys who got the attention he craved growing up. He would flirt with the girls, their boyfriends would get angry and a fight would ensue. Ballinger always won, usually with only one punch, occasionally a second one was required, but that was rare.

Toward the end of his senior year a guidance counselor suggested the military might bring him the discipline and focus he was lacking. He joined the Marines the day after graduation and never looked back.

Ballinger found that the Marines did indeed provide him with the discipline and focus he needed. He also developed a sense of self worth and a love of his country, a love ultimately ruined by kiss-ass officers at the highest levels who never saw a day of combat. They made poor decisions, on a daily basis, costing hundreds of lives, including those of some of his closest friends. His fellow Marines became the family he always wanted but never had. The Marine discipline and focus also turned him into a finely tuned, highly efficient killing machine. It was the perfect release for years of pent up anger and rage over the continual neglect in his life.

He finished the sniper rifle assembly, attached the bi-pod to the barrel just above the stock and gently laid the weapon down like a mother returning a new born to its crib. It would take less than three quarters of a second for the bullet to travel from the top of the Zurich building to the southwest door of the OPEC building.

Chapter Two

Forty- five year old Trinidad Palacios, "Trini" to his friends, had sunken cheekbones, a pointed nose, and stood a shade over six feet. His gaunt frame and lanky stature made his facial features even more prominent. He had a thinning and rapidly receding hairline and wore thick wire rimmed glasses. All in all, he looked like a living caricature of the Ichabod Crane character in Washington Irving's short story about the headless horseman.

A light rain was falling outside as Trini sat at his desk in the study of the family's opulently furnished OPEC apartment. His employers spared no expense when it came to the comforts of home. The spacious apartment had three bedrooms, a gourmet kitchen and expensive antique European furniture dotted every room. The luxurious living quarters were kept clean by a maid who came in twice a week.

The complex included an on-site gym, frequented by his wife to maintain her absolutely perfect figure. Trini often wondered how a man of his looks and body ended up with such a beauty. When he would ask his wife about it she would laugh it off and reply that his inner beauty, caring and sensitivity were all she could ever want in a member of the opposite sex.

The only room not neat and tidy in the entire apartment was Trini's study. It looked like a library that had been hit by a tornado. There were layers of scientific papers on every surface available. The shelves held books stacked every which way imaginable. Mountains of books and papers sat on the floor, abandoned long ago for more up to date publications. A few half empty coffee cups and a dozen or so partially eaten pastries added a moldy touch of color to the chaotic ambience. To anyone else the room looked like a disaster area waiting for the Red Cross to arrive. To Trini it was carefully organized chaos.

He had been up since four a.m. reading all the documents he carried home from his office the night before. Even though he had read them all hundreds of times, he still found it hard to believe. Yet, the truth lay there on his desk, staring up at him like a coiled snake readying to strike. A conspiracy of this magnitude was unfathomable. How could it have happened? Who could have orchestrated it?

There were copies of memos, emails and cables sent to various people from all around the world. Many were from OPEC countries. Individually they didn't point to much at all. But looked at as a whole, it was clear a conspiracy had been carefully and meticulously designed and put into place. Trini spent nearly six months calling in favors, bribing clerks and snooping through computers and trash bins long after ordinary business hours ended. He had carefully assembled all the pieces of the puzzle. The world oil shortage crisis that was growing larger each day was all a sham.

As an analyst for OPEC, one of his main functions was to monitor and report on world oil production. For nearly eight months, several OPEC countries had been cutting oil production and it had peaked Trini's curiosity. It just didn't make sense. Based on previous reports, Trini was confident there were ample amounts of oil, above and below ground, in all the OPEC countries. Yet, the cut back had happened. Saudi Arabia was the first, followed by Iran, Iraq, Venezuela and Kuwait. The results worldwide were disastrous. Europeans already used to paying high prices for their petrol were outraged and U.S. consumers were starting to see prices climb well above five dollars a gallon. Crude oil had reached an all time high of one hundred-seventy dollars a barrel. Many cities in Europe and the U.S. were implementing gas rationing. Banks the world over were repossessing gas guzzling vehicles at an alarming rate. Consumers could no longer afford large car and truck payments equivalent to the cost of a tank of gas.

At first, the larger oil producing countries cut production by five percent. The last set of data showed that some of them had cut production by nearly 20 percent over the previous eight months, and all of them were claiming that several of their wells had run dry.

It appeared that the conspiracy had been put together by some of the people Trini worked with at OPEC. He realized he had to put a stop to the madness. His plan was to make the announcement at the press conference scheduled that afternoon. These press conferences were routine when OPEC meetings were in session. And given the alleged crisis, the world press was eager for any morsel OPEC might offer. While Trini had done his best to cover his tracks and keep his findings a secret, he knew he couldn't be absolutely sure no one else knew about his discovery.

Trini also knew that if he told the higher ups at OPEC he would find himself out on the street, out of a job, and labeled a crackpot in short order. After several long and sleepless nights he felt the best thing, the only thing he could do, was to make the announcement and let the chips fall where they may. If he was going to be out of a job anyway, he was going to go out with a clear conscience.

He picked up the documents, stuffed them into an envelope and addressed it to his old friend and colleague, Garrison Shepherd, in Houston, Texas. Trini and Garrison had worked together at Global Oil in Houston before Trini had landed his dream job at OPEC. They had similar scientific backgrounds and ideas about the future of oil in the world. Trini and Garrison had quickly become good friends and often helped each other on various complex projects they were assigned at Global. Trini figured the information he was sending to Garrison would serve as an insurance policy in the event that something happened. He knew Garrison would do the right thing with the information if it ever came to that. Trini swallowed the last drop of cold coffee from one of the many cups on his desk and hastily scribbled a note to his wife asking her to drop the package off at the Post Office on her way to the market later that day. He made a quick call to Garrison, got his voice mail, and left a message telling him to expect an important package, one they would talk about later in greater detail.

Trini left his apartment at six-forty five that morning, an hour earlier than usual, and headed to his office. Before leaving, he kissed his wife and two sleepy kids goodbye. He assured the entire family that wild horses couldn't keep him from attending his son's soccer match that afternoon and his daughter's ballet recital that evening. The OPEC limo was waiting for him in the circular drive of the residence. The driver, a stocky guy with a sullen scarred face, held the door open as Trini climbed in. The early morning fog was beginning to clear and a glimmer of sun was slowly pushing its way through the heavy cloud cover. It was a day Trini hoped would become brighter still after he made his announcement. The driver climbed in, looked in the rear view mirror and pulled into the light morning traffic. They arrived at OPEC headquarters just past seven.

Trini poured himself a fresh cup of coffee and closed the door to his cluttered office, a close replica of his chaotic home office, right down to the stale pastries. He spent the next two hours rehearsing what he was going to say at the press briefing. He had nothing in writing, everything had been sent to Garrison. He didn't want anyone discovering what he was going to say. He viewed his discovery as a matter of providing economic stability to a world that was rapidly falling apart. Someone had to do something, and he was that someone.

Trini rose from his chair, stood next to his desk, took a deep breath and headed for the door. He walked quickly through the building, with an intense focus on the task at hand. He was a man on a mission, oblivious to the people and things around him. It was exactly ten-fifteen that morning when he walked through the door at the southwest corner of the OPEC building. The limo driver was waiting patiently, holding the door of the vehicle open for his passenger. The destination was the Vienna Hilton where the world press would be given details about the bogus oil shortage. Trini had a clear head and a precise vision of what he was going to say. He was confident he had come to the right decision.

As Trini stepped through the OPEC doorway into the bright sunshine, Ballinger calmly exhaled and squeezed the trigger of the M82A1. At ten-fifteen and three quarters of a second, Trinidad Palacios was no longer among the living. His world had come to a sudden tragic end, his mission unsuccessful. The fifty caliber round had ripped through his chest like a freight train, hitting a portion of his heart before burying itself deep into the concrete wall behind the door. All snipers are taught to aim for center mass, the biggest target with less chance for a miss. The bullet takes care of the rest. Trini didn't make it to the soccer match or the ballet recital, but it wasn't wild horses that kept him away.

Ballinger laid the M82 aside and pulled the Glock from the gym bag. He fired six random shots into cars and shop windows in the street far below. Fear instantly filled the air as panic spread and people fled. No one knew what the actual danger was or where it was coming from, but they instinctively knew they needed to be somewhere else, and the sooner the better.

An elderly woman screamed and dropped her grocery bag. A bottle of milk exploded as it hit the sidewalk. Three oranges and an onion made a dash for the street. A group of school children screamed and ran into a nearby book store.

Ballinger stepped behind the closest HVAC unit where he was totally hidden from view and changed his clothes. He put on a workman's uniform that identified him as Fritz Heitzing from Heitzing Heating Repair. He tucked the Glock into the back of his waistband and pulled his shirt down to cover it. He quickly disassembled the M82, dropped it in the gym bag, zipped it closed and walked to the south edge of the building. Giving careful aim, he dropped the gym bag straight down into the open dumpster below.

Ballinger casually walked back to the north side of the roof, opened the roof hatch, climbed down the ladder and walked down the long hallway to the stairwell. The last thing he did before heading down the stairs was to pull the fire alarm. He snapped off the latex gloves, pulling them inside out and stuffed them in his pants pocket. He casually, but quickly, joined the exiting office workers, blending in perfectly. People were on the verge of panic, but no one ran as they found the exit stairs and hustled down. The sounds of approaching sirens filled the air.

After 12 flights of stairs, he exited the building, looked up at the clear blue sky and headed back towards his hotel. As he walked, he calmly pulled out his cell phone and dialed the Senator's private number in Washington DC. "Done" he said, and hung up. He ripped the burner phone in half and dropped part of it into a trash bin as he made his way down the crowded sidewalk. The other half went into a flooded canal four blocks away.

Chapter Three

The call came in to the Central Intelligence Agency's National Clandestine Service unit in Langley, Virginia, less than an hour later. After the September 11 attacks in 2001, the NCS was raked over the coals by the Senate Select Committee on Intelligence for not having enough data to see the pending threat. Since that time, the NCS quickly jumped on every worldwide event with even the slightest hint of a terrorism connection. The killing of an OPEC analyst clearly raised terrorist concerns. The United States knew that any kind of terrorist incident could have an immediate effect on an already shaky world economy, especially with the rapidly escalating oil crisis.

After regrouping in the aftermath of nine-eleven, the NCE had been instrumental in thwarting several terrorist attacks. They found themselves working with the FBI at home as well as every other imaginable agency in the world. The war on terrorism knew no boundaries. The U.S. agencies who were friendly competitors suddenly found themselves working together. Old animosities were set aside in favor of the common good. Congress was all for the intelligence gathering and had even turned a blind eye to a few borderline operations. Several ranking Congressmen and Senators were eager to take credit when things were going well. Continual snooping of cyberspace, telephone lines and the airwaves seemed to be making the world a safer place.

All the Congressional praise and understanding went south in a hurry when a low level computer geek named Edward Snowden vanished from his job at the NSA one day and reappeared in Russia a few weeks later with a briefcase full of secrets. Despite the diplomatic issues, Russia welcomed Snowden with open arms eager to help discredit its old cold war enemy. The same Congress that took credit for saving the world was now busy pointing fingers and placing blame. They stayed pretty busy patting themselves on the back for protecting the rights of U.S. citizens and disavowing any knowledge of CIA or NSA intelligence gathering. Spying on Americans by Americans simply wasn't acceptable. In fact, it was a travesty of the highest magnitude. Investigations and finger pointing took a front row seat. Political capital was gathered, neatly packaged and put on a shelf for further use at election time.

NCS Deputy Director Allen Blackwell sat in his office staring out the window at the late fall colors. His office was tastefully decorated and functional. It lacked the grandiose opulence shown by others at his level. Unlike them, he didn't have an inflated ego that constantly needed to be fed, he was comfortable with who he was. A large, fairly new, oak desk was the office center piece. The desk was covered with a variety of papers and files. A gold framed picture of his wife and kids occupied one corner. It sat next to a small sailboat made of brass atop a diminutive piece of marble. There were two typical government-issued chairs with leather seats and backs facing the desk. In one corner of the room, an oak coffee table was sandwiched between a small couch and two other leather chairs. A variety of pictures dotted one wall showing Blackwell with various political figures from both parties. Another wall was filled with sailboat posters and pictures of the Deputy sailing on the Potomac with various friends and colleagues.

He took the call from the Director of INTERPOL who gave him the details of the Palacios assassination. Blackwell was a pensive man known for his patience and excellent analytical skills. He had broad shoulders and more than one scar on his lean body from various covert operations he participated in over the years. He had spent his time in the trenches, paid his dues and had the political savvy needed to slip into an administrative role as his body weakened. He wore stylish, black-rimmed glasses. They were accentuated by his salt and pepper hair that began appearing when he reached the downhill side of fifty. White shirts and gray suits with expensive Hermes ties made up his entire wardrobe.

Blackwell directed several questions into the phone as he sipped coffee from his University of Oregon cup. Oregon was his alma mater where he had majored in world history. The CIA had recruited him right out of college. It had been a typical rainy Oregon day with student radicals picketing the CIA's presence on campus when he was interviewed. He had never held a job anywhere else. That cup was his prize possession from his old Oregon days.

The questions he asked were the typical who, what, when, where, why and how. The CIA had a long and amicable relationship with INTERPOL. They had each helped the other a number of times over the years. The who, what and when were easily answered by INTERPOL. The how would come in a matter of hours. The why was never easily answered, hence the cooperation and involvement of the NCS. Blackwell hung up after promising to keep in touch as the case evolved.

In the late seventies, the CIA established a covert group of private contractors for jobs that needed discretion to keep the agency out of the spotlight. They were the kind of contractors you never heard about, and didn't want to know about. Referred to as Looking Glass, they were paid from a special fund that showed up as a research and development line in the CIA budget. Looking Glass operatives were a hodgepodge of former Navy Seals, Special Forces and CIA operatives. The assassination of Palacios clearly mandated an investigation that called for discretion, especially in the current political climate. Blackwell opened the safe in his office and removed the Looking Glass file with the operatives' names and areas of expertise. He chewed on his lower lip as his eyes scrolled down the list.

Jack Wilder's name and background quickly caught his eye. A veteran of many clandestine operations and one of the agency's former top operatives, he had all the skills needed for the assignment. Wilder was what one would call average in physical stature and looks. He had brackish brown hair and blue eyes. He was good looking by most standards but definitely not the type you'd see modeling clothes in GQ magazine. Nothing about him stood out that would give the average person reason to pay any attention to him. He was a trim one-eighty and stood just over five-ten. At forty years old he was physically fit and could run five miles with little effort. He had served time in the Army Special Forces and had taken part in joint covert CIA-Special Forces operations a number of times. It was a natural fit when the CIA recruited him away from Special Forces.

After several years at the agency Jack had become disillusioned at the constant CYA attitude that had evolved. Paranoia about Congress kept getting in the way of getting things done, important things. He'd finally had enough and was ready to leave the agency when Blackwell steered him to the Looking Glass Group. There was no CYA attitude, no Congressional oversight to deal with. The only thing that mattered was getting the job done. There were no worries about legal parameters or constitutional rights to get in the way. The downside was if any of them were ever caught, they would immediately be disavowed and erased from the CIA system. For Jack, it was all a risk well worth taking.

Blackwell knew that Wilder had just returned from an oil related assignment in the Middle East and figured if there was any kind of terrorist connection, Jack would be the one most likely to uncover it. He knew Wilder to be intelligent, cautious and able to push the envelope when the situation called for it. Jack was always able to get results. Blackwell also knew Wilder to be somewhat of a ladies' man who liked his liquor. Although it had raised a few eyebrows on more than one occasion, it never interfered with his getting the job done.

An hour later a casual Wilder arrived in Blackwell's office. He wore a yellow polo shirt that accentuated his recently acquired Middle East tan, blue jeans and cordovan loafers.

"The Middle East sun seems to agree with you," Blackwell commented.

"Helps to blend in with the locals," Jack replied.

Blackwell offered Jack coffee which he declined and began to describe the situation and what needed to be done.

"You're not going to believe this, but I knew this Palacios guy," Wilder said. "I met him about six months ago in Houston at a friend's wedding. He and his wife had flown in from Vienna for the event. Turns out my friend who was getting married and Palacios had worked together for several years at Global Oil in Houston. Palacios was apparently some kind of super genius oil analyst before he was recruited away from Global by OPEC. I think he was originally from Venezuela, small world."

"Wow, pretty weird" Blackwell said." Be that as it may, just gather up whatever resources you need and get started as quickly as you can. The U.S. has a serious interest in OPEC and their oil. Any kind of a crisis that comes out of this could put some heavy pressure on our oil production and reserves."

Blackwell leaned back in his chair, took a sip of coffee that had grown cold, and looked up at the ceiling.

"If this is something more than a nut job with a gun, like someone from outside Austria, it could turn into an international can of worms in an instant. And one last thing that goes without saying, if anything in this operation goes sideways; you know you're on your own. We have no knowledge of who you are or what you're doing."

"Sure," Jack said, "It's always good to know my old friends at the agency are the first ones to throw me under the bus when things get tough."

"Happy to be of service," Blackwell said.

As Jack headed back to the parking lot his thoughts turned to November of the previous year when Trini Palacios and his wife Inez had come from Vienna to Houston to attend Garrison Shepherd's wedding. Jack and Garrison had been close friends for over thirty years. Jack recalled the wedding and remembered Inez Palacios as being incredibly attractive. A former Venezuelan beauty contestant, she turned heads at the wedding in her smooth fitting, pale green silk dress. The outfit was made even more stunning by her long dark hair, smooth olive skin and dark brown eyes. She walked with an air of grace and confidence through the room, meeting and shaking hands with other guests. Her husband, on the other hand, seemed to be withdrawn and preoccupied. He didn't say much the whole evening. Jack remembered thinking *what an odd match up the two of them seemed to be.*

Jack went to the fridge in his small, sparse apartment and grabbed a Corona. The apartment consisted of one blandly furnished bedroom, a small kitchen adjacent to a living room and a simple bathroom off the bedroom. The furnishings were all items purchased from second-hand stores in the area. Over the years, Jack realized all he really needed was a place to sleep. He had spent most of his life traveling and living out of hotels and military accommodations all over the world. A large fifty inch television took up most of one wall in the living room. A leather sofa sat opposite the TV behind a beat up coffee table with stains and spills that looked like they'd been there for years. The only other item of furniture in the room was an old leather recliner with well worn arms and a broken foot rest. A tall reading lamp stood next to the recliner. An old book case full of books on world history sat next to the reading lamp. Jack picked up a lime, sliced a wedge out of it and shoved it down the neck of the Corona bottle as he sat down on the old sofa.

He took a swig of the Corona and thought about his longtime friend Garrison Shepherd. Garrison had always been the serious one. Jack had always been the clown. They both started college at the same time. Jack recalled the time the CIA had come to their college campus on a recruiting trip. As usual, there were a group of students standing out in front of the Student Union Building protesting the CIA's presence on campus. As Garrison walked by, he got it into his head that protesters had no right to protest the fact that jobs were being offered to fellow students. He sat his books down, calmly walked up to the loudest protestor, indicated his displeasure with the guy's protest and promptly smacked the guy in the mouth. The picture on the front page of the student newspaper the next day was the back of Garrison as he was walking away. The caption read "Mystery student protests protestors with fist sandwich." Nothing ever came of it because it all happened in an instant and no one knew who Garrison was.

Four years later, Garrison graduated with an engineering degree. Three universities, two wives and six years after that, Jack graduated with a degree in psychology. He had married wife number two while he was busy cramming a four year curriculum into 11 years. The marriage was doomed from the beginning. She had come from money and Jack had come from Clown College. Early one morning, after a particularly brutal argument with his wife and too much to drink the night before, a hung over Jack stormed out of the house and found himself wandering around a strip mall. He noticed a huge

Army recruiting poster hanging in a window. The byline of the poster read *"The U.S. Army, your ticket to adventure."* Jack saw it as a one way ticket out of his marriage. He walked in, signed the papers and never looked back.

At age 24 he was one of the oldest guys in his boot camp class. Halfway through boot camp at Fort Bliss in El Paso, Texas he was served with divorce papers, which he gladly signed and returned. The divorce papers essentially gave everything to his wife. To Jack, it was a small price to pay for his freedom.

Garrison's wedding had truly been an affair to remember, lots of drinking, and dancing. Jack had spent the night in his hotel room with one of the bridesmaids. He had given a short, but heartfelt toast to the bride and groom just before turning his attention to Celeste Windom, the best looking of all the bridesmaids. It was clearly lust at first sight. Jack was mesmerized. There was radiance about Celeste that Jack simply couldn't take his eyes off of, or it may have been her more than ample bust line accentuated by the low-cut bridesmaid dress she wore. He'd insisted on toasting her as well. "Here's to the little things in life" he said, "here's to your little thing and here's to my little thing, and just remember, if your little thing ever needs anything, my little thing isn't doing anything." Then he turned back to Garrison, raised his eyebrows, grinned like a Cheshire cat and winked at Garrison as he made his way to Celeste's table.

Celeste Windom was about five-four with blonde hair, blue eyes, dimples that accentuated her great smile and a slightly turned up nose. She had a degree in computer science and had grown up in Denver with two brothers, one older and one younger. She held her own with everyone when it came to downing shots of tequila at the bridesmaids' table. She was also one of the most self assured women Jack had ever met. Ah yes, a night to remember.

Jack booked himself on a red eye flight to Houston. The plan was to connect with his old friend Garrison to try and get some inside information on what Trini's job had been at OPEC. Jack's cat, Angus, impatiently brushed against Jack's leg while he was on the phone making his travel arrangements. "Hang tight bud, I'll be with you in a minute," Jack said to the fur ball. "I need to pack a bag first." With the exception of Garrison Shepherd and a CIA colleague who died a few years back, Angus was the closest thing to a friend Jack had. One day a few years earlier, as Jack opened the door to his apartment, the cat appeared from out of nowhere and made a beeline straight for Jack's couch. Jack opened the fridge, took out a beer, and poured half in a dish for the cat. They had been drinking buddies ever since. They shared the occasional can of tuna, but it was mostly the beer and the conversation that made for a perfect friendship. Angus was a great listener. He may have had a small drinking problem, but it never interfered with his ability to listen to Jack's problems, and he always seemed to agree with what Jack was saying.

Jack finished packing, fed Angus, opened a beer and sat down on the couch to think. He finished most of his beer and poured what was left into the cat's dish. He picked his Walther PPK .380 off the hall tree along with his shoulder holster and two spare clips that fit into pockets on either side of the holster. He grabbed two more clips, his Glock 26 back-up, his ankle holster for the 26, and tucked the whole lot into his suitcase. Jack gave Angus a nod. Angus seemed to nod back in his own little intoxicated way. "See ya later buddy, there's plenty of beer in the fridge if you get thirsty," he said as he patted the top of the cat's head and walked out the door. He took a cab to the airport and called his neighbor, Mrs. Dickenson, on the way and asked her to look after Angus.

Chapter Four

Thirty-five-year-old Garrison Shepherd was a sports nut. He loved to watch sports and he loved to play sports. At five foot-nine inches and a hundred-sixty pounds he wasn't the best athlete in the many over thirty co-ed leagues he played in, but he wasn't the worst either. He had dark hair graying around the temples and wore thick glasses. He was, by some standards, what you could call handsome, in an intellectual sort of way. Not a movie star kind of handsome, but a lot of women would still give him a second look in a crowded room. He never noticed the first look, let alone the second one. His thoughts were always elsewhere, usually on work.

Aside from playing and watching sports, Garrison's greatest passion was his job at Global Oil. What others found boring, he found fascinating. He was often at the office on weekends, not because he needed to be there, but because he wanted to be there. Looking at data, analyzing the data, then, telling his employers where to look for their next big oil score. What could be more fun?

Then, eight months ago, another passion came into Garrison's life in the form of five feet- one inch Angelina Bishop. Their paths connected at Starbucks. Garrison was sitting with his running buddies after a five mile Saturday run. As usual the place was packed, not an empty table to be found. Angelina appeared in the doorway. She wore blue running shorts, a yellow running shirt and red running shoes.

All Nike, all expensive. Garrison couldn't take his eyes off her. He watched as she made her way through the crowd to the counter. She ordered a tall, skinny decaf vanilla latte. *Decaf* he thought to himself, *what's the point?* As she surveyed the crowded room, Garrison stood and motioned her over to an empty seat at their table, the only empty seat in the place. At first she pretended not to notice. She held herself somewhat aloof and continued to look around. It was almost as if she was looking for a better offer for a seating companion. Garrison got up and walked over to her. "If you're looking for a place to sit, we would be happy to have you join us."

"Sure," she said as she followed him back to his table.

"I'm Garrison," he said as he held out his hand.

"Angelina," she replied, as she took his hand somewhat half heartedly. Introductions were made all around. Garrison's friends all went back to their various conversations giving Garrison the opportunity to chat with his new friend.

"Do you come here often?" he asked. "I haven't seen you here before."

"I just moved here a week ago, got tired of unpacking boxes and decided to go for a run and ended up here."

They sat and talked long after Garrison's running mates had gone. Garrison found out that she had recently moved to Houston from Chicago. She had been married to an older man who made his fortune in the Chicago real estate market and passed away from a sudden heart attack nearly a year ago. After spending several months dealing with the estate and getting things settled, she had become restless and in need of a change. She had sold the lavish home in Chicago and moved to Houston.

Much to the consternation of the running group, Garrison invited her to run with them on Saturdays. Each Saturday the run would end at Starbucks. Each Saturday Garrison's friends would like her less and Garrison would like her more. They all saw her as an overbearing, aloof, gold digger, only concerned about money. She often mentioned the luxuries she had while she lived in Chicago.

Despite the group's warnings, Garrison's naiveté kept him from seeing what they were seeing. For her part, Angelina introduced Garrison to opera, ballet, museums, expensive clothes and fine dining in trendy restaurants. She even talked him into joining the local country club. Three months later Garrison Mansfield Shepherd and Angelina Annetta Bishop were joined together in holy matrimony. When the preacher said "If there is anyone who thinks these two should not be joined together speak now or forever hold your peace," there were about fifty people who considered raising their hands, but none did.

Chapter Five

Garrison and Angelina were in the den of their new lavish Houston home watching the end of the Oregon - St. Louis basketball game in the NCAA tournament when his cell phone rang. It looked like Oregon was finally going to make it into the Sweet Sixteen and Garrison, a diehard Oregon fan, was on the edge of his seat cheering and drinking an expensive imported beer. Angelina was just entering the cool down mode on her exercise bike. Garrison looked at the caller ID. It was Inez Palacios calling from Vienna. He looked at his watch; it was six p.m., three a.m. Vienna time. Not good.

He immediately forgot the game, muted the TV and answered.

"Inez, is everything okay?" he asked as he pressed the phone to his ear.

"Garrison, something terrible has happened. Trini has been killed." Garrison's mind began to race. What had happened, an automobile crash, some kind of freak accident? He and Trini were very close when they worked together at Global Oil. Trini had been a great mentor to him. They would often talk about the data they were working on long into the night over a beer or glass of wine. He remembered what a great time Trini and Inez had at his wedding. "What was it, what happened?"

"He was shot, it happened at work. He was just leaving his office to give the weekly briefing to the press. Someone shot him as he stepped out of the building." Garrison's mind raced even faster. He pictured some crazed gunman in the crowd who had become fed up with high gasoline prices and had gone over the edge and started shooting up the place.

"Inez, who was it, did they catch him?"

"They don't know, Garrison. The police think someone may have shot him from several blocks away, from the top of some building. I think it may have had something to do with his work. For the past couple of weeks he was very quiet, like something was bothering him. He wasn't his usual self. When I would ask what the problem was, he would just say it was some issues at work." Inez sounded very tired and distraught. "Garrison, have you heard from Trini at all? If it were something technical at work, I'm sure he would have called you. The two of you were such a great team at Global Oil. He was always talking about how smart you are and what a great future you have at Global."

"He did call a couple of days ago and left a rather cryptic message on my cell phone, something about needing to talk about some data he had discovered. He said he was sending me a copy to look over. Angelina and I were out of town for a few days backpacking in Colorado and didn't have cell coverage. We got home late last night. That's when I realized he had left me a message. I haven't received the data he said he was going to send. I thought maybe he changed his mind. I've been holding off on calling because of the time difference. I was going to call him early tomorrow morning, Houston time."

"I still have the package Garrison, Trini asked me to send it. With all that has happened, I forgot about it. I will get it out to you soon. If it is something about his work and it's important I am sure he wanted you to know about it."

"Inez, you sound exhausted. Why don't you try and get some rest. I'll make a call later to some of the people I know at OPEC to see what I can find out. I'll call you in a day or so, as soon as I have some news. Tell the kids hi and give them a hug for me."

"Who was that?" Angelina asked as Garrison hung up. She had been so engrossed in the game she hadn't paid any attention to the phone conversation.

"It was Inez in Vienna. Trini has been killed."

"Oh," she said "I'm going to the kitchen to get a glass of wine would you care for some"? *That's a little cold*, Garrison thought to himself, *but then I guess that's just Angelina.*

"No thanks," he said. "I'm going to bed."

Garrison had a sleepless night. He kept going over and over things in his mind to see if he could come up with any reason someone would want to kill his friend. He also spent time thinking about Angelina's coldness. It didn't make sense. He knew she didn't care for many of his friends. Still, he expected a little sympathy. He decided he would confront her about it soon. He hated confrontation of any kind, but this was something that needed to be discussed.

The next day was Saturday, a day to run. He'd slept a little later than usual and didn't feel like running. He made himself a cup of coffee and sat at the kitchen table trying to sort through everything he had heard from Inez. None of it made sense. Angelina's callous attitude certainly didn't help. She had gotten up earlier and left a note on the fridge. She said she was going shopping. The more he thought about it all, the more muddled it became. What had Trini been working on? What was in the package of data that he had asked Inez to send? Who would want to kill Trini and why? The longer he sat, the more perplexed and confused he became.

Garrison decided to go for a run after all. Maybe a good run would help clear his head. He still couldn't get his mind around what had happened to Trini. It just didn't make any sense. Why would anyone want to kill his friend? He was a half hour behind his running mates, but with a quick pace he would have plenty of time to meet up with them at Starbucks. He put on his running gear and jogged out the door, taking his usual route.

The temperature was in the low sixties and the usual Houston humidity had taken the day off, a great day for a run. He lengthened his stride and took deeper breaths. All the muddled thoughts in his head were beginning to clear a little. As he focused on his breathing and his running, he didn't notice the black Mercedes with the heavily tinted windows that slowly followed him as he ran along Lions Club Lake on the far side of Bane Park, the most desolate part of his route.

It was a bright, sunny, cloudless day with a cool five mile an hour breeze blowing in from the gulf. Officer Trotter was just wrapping up a call on a domestic dispute in a rundown apartment complex on Dillon Street, a few blocks from Houston's Hobby airport. It had been a typical domestic call. An argument had gotten out of hand and the guy had smacked his wife. No blood, just a badly bruised cheek. A neighbor heard the yelling and called the cops. Trotter had been there twice before. He was beginning to feel like family. He had really wanted to take the guy in. Actually, he had really wanted to shoot the guy, but there were some pretty strict rules about that sort of thing. As usual, the wife refused to press charges. "He really didn't mean to do it," she said with a split lip. They were both kissing and hugging when Trotter finally broke away and walked back to his patrol car. Dispatch called just as he got behind the wheel.

"Victor seven-seven, possible homicide corner of Airport Boulevard and Tewantin Drive. Caller says he found a body in a field."

"Victor seven-seven in En route," Trotter responded, as he hit the switch for lights and siren.

Shawn Trotter looked like most officers on the force. His reddish blonde hair was cut Marine short. He had a fair, clean shaven complexion and came in at about five-ten and one seventy-five. His bulky Kevlar vest made him look a little rounder than he really was. He had a distinctive walk, not what you would call a swagger, rather a gait of confidence. He had gone to Bible College and spent time as a youth pastor before joining the police force. College was where he picked up his calming demeanor. He showed a high level of respect for those he dealt with in the field - good guys and bad guys alike - even though at times all he wanted was to rip the bad guys to pieces.

As a youth pastor Trotter had been concerned about the various evils and temptations available on every corner, just itching to ruin young lives. He soon realized his true ministerial calling was to fight evil on the front lines, and that was what he had been doing for the past 10 years as a Patrol Officer for the Houston PD. And now, here he was, in an empty barren field, staring down at the body of a guy who appeared to have been shot several times in the back and the back of the head. In 10 years he had seen many bodies. Some had died from natural causes, others in tragic accidents. But somehow, a murder always seemed to hit him a little harder. True evil had once again reared its ugly head and was on the march. No one deserved to die by being shot in the back.

Kyle Granger and his eight year old son Joshua had been flying their Trilby kites in a field just south of Hobby Airport where there was nearly always a stiff breeze. Kite flying had become a Sunday father-son tradition that provided Kyle some quality time with Joshua. It was also time to decompress after a long hectic week in the office of the large accounting firm where Kyle worked. In the field, he could unwind and enjoy the fresh air and sunshine while having fun with his son. The two of them had discovered this field six months earlier and quickly realized it was the perfect kite flying venue. The terrain was a little rough, but mostly free of rocks, trees and other kite snagging dragons.

It just doesn't get better than this, Kyle thought as he watched Josh running at full speed unwinding the spool of string as he went. Josh had glanced down at the ground in front of him and had seen something that looked like a scarecrow. His mind told him to stop, but his feet didn't quite get the message. Forward momentum was in charge; he had tripped and gone flying over the body landing head first in the dirt.

Trotter slowly backed away from the body, separated the two kite flyers, and took statements from each of them. He carefully surveyed the scene and retrieved the famous yellow tape from the trunk of his squad car. He saw what looked like two drag marks from the street to where the body lay in the field. He started across the street from the field and cordoned off an area about thirty feet on either side of

42

the drag marks and about thirty feet past the body. His Sergeant and a homicide detective arrived just as he was finishing up with the tape.

Detective Stan Bonham had been on the force forever. His hair was nearly all gray and thinning. He had a light tan and a weathered face that had seen far too many homicides in his career. His deep set blue eyes gave the surroundings a quick look. He grabbed a role of red tape from his car and had Trotter set up a second smaller perimeter closer to the body, the red zone. He then showed Trotter where he wanted the ingress and egress routes established. Trotter knew the drill. He would stay as long as he was needed, logging each person in and out of the red zone to protect the integrity of the crime scene.

Bonham put on a pair of latex gloves, entered the red zone and squatted down to have a closer look at the body. The deceased was thin with a runner's build, wearing yellow Nike running shoes, dark blue running shorts and a red Nike shirt. He was lying face down in the dirt. Bonham counted what looked like four bullet holes in his back and one in the back of his head. The detective carefully unzipped the small pocket on the back of the dead guy's Nike running shorts and pulled out a driver's license. The ID read Garrison Shepherd, the address was on Tangley Street in the West University neighborhood. "Well Mr. Shepherd," Bonham said to the dank air, "you're a long way from home. How the hell did you end up way over here with several bullet holes in your back?"

Chapter Six

At long last Angelina had a feeling of freedom.
Garrison had been a nice guy and all, but she felt
smothered by him. He was so clingy, always wanting
to do things for her. Her first husband was also nice.
Nice and rich, but at least he wasn't clingy. He had
always stayed busy with his wheeling and dealing in
Chicago real estate and left her alone most of the
time. She had been the perfect trophy wife that he
called upon once in awhile to accompany him to
some high roller event. Arm candy like that was the
envy of many of his wealthy colleagues. She was fine
with that. The benefits far outweighed the misery of
putting up with the old guy. Benefits like shopping
for expensive clothes, eating at the finest restaurants,
and going to the best spas for facials, manicures and
massages.

To Angelina it had been the perfect marriage and
probably would have stayed perfect if her wealthy
husband hadn't come home a day early from his latest
business trip. Her husband, Bardwell Bishop, "The
Bard" to his friends, was a good provider, but a poor
lover. He was 20 years older than she was. He looked
like that cartoon character guy you see on the
Monopoly board game. He had a pale, ruddy face
with a slightly enlarged reddish nose from too much
drinking, and a big bushy white mustache. His taste
for fine food and wine had pushed him close to
portly. Rather than trying to lose weight, he simply
bought bigger clothes. Just like the Monopoly
character from the board game, he always held his

hand out to shake yours. He was constantly searching for that connection to his next big deal. There was certainly no big deal to close when it came to bedroom romance. It was wham, bam, rollover and go to sleep. He was a far cry from Clay, the one she was in bed with when he came home from Philadelphia a day early.

Angelina had discovered Clay at the gym and invited him over for a drink one afternoon while Bardwell was away on one of his many business trips. Although she thought of herself as being pretty fit, she was no match for Clay. Their lengthy love making sessions left her exhausted. She found it hard to keep up with his insatiable desire but did her best. It was just one of those sacrifices you make for someone who would do anything for you.

When he wasn't in the sack with Angelina, Clay was working out at the gym, constantly looking at himself in the mirrored gym wall. He was the perfect stereotype of a television California surfer dude. He had blonde hair, blue eyes, a deep tan bulging with muscles and the IQ of a rock.

At first her Bardwell was angry and asked how long the affair had been going on. Then he just pouted for a couple of days and slept in one of the five spare bedrooms. Finally he said he had made a decision and she needed to leave. He told her his attorney would be in touch and work things out, and that she would be well taken care of. He was already thinking of ways to make a move on the new young secretary in his office. She wasn't as attractive as Angelina, but still pretty enough to attract his attention and he could tell she was mesmerized by his money and power. Angelina took the whole thing very calmly and said she needed a week to find another place to live. He agreed to let her stay.

A few days later, Bardwell had his unfortunate heart attack while having drinks at the posh Mid-America Club located on the eightieth floor of the Aon building in downtown Chicago. It was a Friday evening and, as was his custom, Bardwell had joined several of his friends for a casual drink to end the week. The bright sun was quickly fading turning daylight to dusk making way for the colorful lights of Chicago. Bardwell was accompanied by a tall stranger whom he introduced as Gregory Allen, a potential new client from Denver. Bardwell took a sip of his drink and glanced out the window at the magnificent view. It was a sight he never tired of. The Bard explained that he was showing Allen some of the sights in Chicago.

Gregory Allen was an alias the killer often used when he was on a job. In everyday life in the seedy underworld of Chicago mobsters, he was known as Subtle. It was a nickname he had picked up over the years because of the subtle and quiet ways he "eliminated problems" for his clients. When it came to hit men for hire, he was one of the best. The deaths of most of his victims had been listed by coroners all around the country as either heart attacks or natural causes.

As they all sat down to enjoy their drinks, Allen used his right hand to adjust the cuff on the left sleeve of his shirt. He removed the dropper from the sleeve and deposited its contents into Bardwell's glass as he picked it up and handed it to Bardwell. He palmed the empty dropper in his right hand and put it in his pocket as he picked up his own glass with his left and bumped it against Bardwell's as if making a toast.

This was a move he had practiced for hours on end to make it look natural. He had used it successfully on many of his victims. After taking a sip of his own drink, Allen excused himself and went to the men's room. A few seconds later when Bardwell stood up, his friends thought it was to take in the breathtaking panoramic view of Chicago. They quickly realized that wasn't the case when he clutched his chest, dropped his drink and fell to the floor.

Living up to his name and reputation, Gregory Allen subtly slipped out the door in the ensuing chaos as a crowd gathered around the gasping Bardwell. The wealthy Bardwell Bishop took his last breath and left the land of the living in the ambulance on the way to Northwestern Memorial. He was dead on arrival. Bardwell had a history of heart problems so no one really questioned anything when *"the big one"* came. They talked about what a great man he was and how much he would be missed. Everyone had forgotten about the tall stranger.

The heart attack, of course, made Angelina a very wealthy widow. The widow who said no to an autopsy being done and immediately had the body cremated. Proud person that he was, the Bard never mentioned his wife's indiscretions to any of his friends. All his wealthy friends were aghast when they learned he hadn't the foresight to get a pre-nup. It was soon afterwards that Angelina made the move to Houston. She was quickly forgotten by Bardwell's friends as they all returned to their lifestyles of the rich and famous.

It had been nearly a year since Bardwell's death and nearly a week since Garrison's. Angelina was sitting on the couch sipping the last of her martini when Jack called. "Hi Ange, it's Jack." Jack Wilder called Angelina, Ange because he knew it pissed her off, and that somehow gave him a warped sense of satisfaction. Of all Garrison's friends, Jack was the one who liked Angelina the least. He had never taken a liking to her, but he was always polite and well mannered when Garrison was around. He knew it wasn't a good match from the start, and could only end badly. He also knew Garrison, and as his best friend, it wasn't up to him to dish out advice on the subject of marriage. One of the reasons Jack didn't like Angelina, was that she reminded him of his former wife. She also had that special charming quality of cold uncaring aloofness. "Is Garrison around?" he asked. "I was thinking he and I might go out for a drink and catch up on things."

"Oh Jack, uh, um, I guess I should have called you. Jack I'm afraid I have some bad news…… Garrison died last week. The funeral is tomorrow."

You cold hearted bitch, Jack thought to himself, as he felt his anger rising to a boiling point. If he could've reached through the phone he would have grabbed her by the neck and joyfully choked the life out of her. He sat stunned and silent for a few seconds trying to put things in perspective. *How could she have not called me? Garrison was one of my best friends and she knew it.* Garrison had made a point of telling her about Jack and their long close friendship at the wedding rehearsal dinner just six months earlier. Jack knew if he stayed on the phone much longer he would say something he would regret. "See you at the funeral" he said, as he squeezed the phone shut. He continued to squeeze the phone, with an image in his mind of his hands around Angelina's neck.

Garrison Shepherd, you bastard, Jack said to himself, *what have you gone and done now?*

Chapter Seven

It was just before midnight on a Thursday when a very drunk Jack Wilder knocked on Celeste Windom's door. He hadn't seen her since Garrison's wedding six months earlier, but they had spoken several times. In addition to seeing Garrison, Jack had planned on rekindling his romance with the former bridesmaid. There was something about her that he just couldn't let go of, and the attraction seemed mutual. At Garrison's wedding after several dances and several glasses of champagne, accompanied by several shots of Jose Cuervo tequila, the two of them had spent a wild and passionate night in Jack's hotel room. The satisfying bliss of lust fulfilled.

"Garrison's dead," Jack said, "and that bitch wife of his wasn't even going to call me." With that, he walked across the spinning room and passed out on the couch.

"And hello to you too," Celeste said to the lump on the couch as she walked past Jack on her way back to bed.

The next morning Jack and his splitting headache woke to the smell of coffee brewing. Celeste was sitting at the table reading the morning paper, waiting for the coffee to finish perking. "You look like a horse that's been rode hard and put away wet," she said.

"You, on the other hand, look as terrific as ever," Jack replied as he poured himself the first cup of coffee and filled her empty cup. He wasn't kidding. Celeste was terrific, and not just in bed. Of all the women he had been with, and there had been many, she was by far the best. She was kind, sensitive, intelligent and attractive. She had what Jack called a magnetic personality. She had soft delicate features, but wasn't afraid to roll up her sleeves and get her hands dirty. She was a software engineer for a big Houston software company. Unlike most computer programmers, she actually had a personality and social skills too. She was outgoing and funny and knew what she wanted out of life. Jack couldn't take his eyes off her at the wedding reception six months ago, and now he was once again mesmerized, drawn to that magnetic personality. As she sat there in her housecoat sipping coffee, Jack couldn't help but wonder what she was wearing underneath the thin robe. Something about this woman drove him crazy.

"Jack, did Angelina really not call you about Garrison?" Celeste said. "We all thought that if she was going to call anyone it would have been you."

"No, it was just a fluke that I found out. I arrived late last night and called Garrison to see if he wanted to go out for a drink to catch up. Angelina answered the phone, stammered a little bit then told me Garrison was dead. What happened to him? I was so mad I didn't even ask her."

"He was murdered Jack, she didn't tell any of us. We read about it in the newspaper and called each other. They found his body in a field near the edge of town, near Hobby Field. The newspaper said he had been shot several times. The whole thing came as a terrible shock to all of us."

Jack felt like someone had kicked him in the stomach. His best friend hadn't just died, he had been murdered. "Was it a mugging or some kind of robbery?" Jack asked.

"No one knows, the police aren't saying anything."

Jack's thoughts turned to his Walther PPK. He imagined putting a bullet or two into Garrison's killer. He would probably put one in the leg for a little suffering and casual information gathering, and a second to the elbow if information wasn't forthcoming. Then he would put one in the head to efficiently finish the job.

Jack finished his coffee and headed for the shower. His emotions were running wild as he stood in Celeste's shower with his palms pressed up against the wall in front of him, the hot water running down his neck and back. In his many years as a CIA Looking Glass operative he had seen and been involved in some pretty scary stuff, but his training had always kept him clear headed and on task. He was always able to focus, no matter what was happening around him. Missions were accomplished, sometimes with casualties, but the operatives never lost focus. Mistakes on an op were a rare occurrence. He knew that letting emotions and feelings run wild was the same as painting a target on your back. He had seen good men die because they weren't thinking clearly in the heat of the battle. Anger in an operation was a clear shortcut to a casket. He couldn't afford to let feelings of anger and revenge get in the way of what he needed to do. He was going to use every resource he had to track down his best friend's killer. And he still had to deal with the OPEC assassination issue. He wondered what the connection between the two murders might be, if any.

After a few minutes the hot water began to loosen his tense muscles. He was finally starting to relax a little and his headache was nearly gone. Celeste stepped in the shower and wrapped her arms tightly around him. He felt her firm warm breasts press against his back. They stood that way for a while, the warm water soothing both their bodies and washing away part of the pain. She slipped her soapy hands down to the front of his thighs. He turned to face her. He put his right hand on the back of her head and pulled her lips to his. He cupped her breast with his left hand. They didn't need a bed, the shower worked out well for what they each had in mind.

Chapter Eight

It was a damp, dreary day when they arrived at the funeral. The sun was obscured by dark brooding clouds, the temperature, dropping like a rock. Jack looked up at the rapidly darkening western sky. Heavy clouds punctuated by sporadic flashes of lightning and rolling thunder announced the storm's imminent arrival. It was coming their way, like Sherman's march to the sea. The dreariness engulfed Jack's entire body, like a giant black pillow trying to suffocate him.

The simple service was held in the First Presbyterian Church, a large building with high ceilings. Stained glass windows ran the full length of the building on either side of the solemn sanctuary. Garrison's ornate coffin held center stage at the front of the gathering. Celeste sat with Garrison's running friends. Several of Garrison's friends from work congregated near the front. Jack sat in the last row as far away from Angelina as he could get. The minister, a short, thin looking fellow, wearing an ugly, ill fitting toupee, opened the service with a prayer. He looked like an old worn out Texas cowboy who had probably spent time on the rodeo circuit, riding bulls and such. The old guy read Garrison's obituary with his slow, Texan drawl, after which the small melodious choir sang "I'll Fly Away."

Jack watched Angelina before the service started. She was sitting in the front row talking on her cell phone, laughing casually at some unheard conversation. As he watched her yakking away, he had a thought - *What about a double funeral?* He could stroll down the aisle to the front row, go over to Angelina, snap her neck and throw her in the coffin alongside Garrison before anyone could grab him. *Hell*, he thought, *I'd probably get a huge applause on the way back to my seat.*

As he sat there in the solemn sanctuary, Jack reflected on another close friend's death some years before. Joaquin Nurillo, Jock, as everybody called him, was the son of Cuban immigrants. He grew up in an affluent suburb of Miami, graduated from Florida State University and went straight to work for the CIA. He and Jack had gone through various CIA trainings together and had worked on several covert operations over the years. For some reason they just hit it off, it was like they totally understood each other. Jock was the younger brother Jack never had, but always wanted.

Jock had been a devilishly handsome guy with an equally devilish charming personality to go with his looks. His Latin features, the dark mysterious eyes, and sometimes over-the-top Latin accent were a definite turn on for the ladies. Young shapely beautiful women couldn't resist him, and unless he was working, he couldn't resist them. He seemed to have a new girlfriend every month.

A few years back, Jock and his girlfriend of the month, an alleged flight attendant for Air France named Christelle, were glissading on the Mount

Adams Glacier in Washington State. After several hours of sliding on the ice and snow, they came to a particularly steep slope. Jock tightened his crampons, got a firm grip on his ice axe and slowly started side stepping down the precipitous slope, as the French beauty watched from above. The mid morning sun had softened the top layer of snow. About forty feet down, the footing gave way and Jock began to slide. He tried desperately to self-arrest with the pick of his ice axe but couldn't get it to take hold. His left foot hit a rock snapping his tibia and catapulting him head over heels into the air. As he somersaulted down the slope like a huge out of control ragdoll snowball, the head of his axe planted itself in the ice and he fell on the spike. Each roll pushed the spike end deeper into his midsection. When he finally came to a stop, he was totally impaled. The climbing tool designed to save him had killed him.

It had taken the rescue party several hours to reach the couple. Jock had been dead for quite awhile before they got to him. There were a bevy of beauties at Jock's funeral, but the French flight attendant was nowhere to be seen. A subtle check by the CIA showed that Air France had no knowledge of any employee matching Christelle's name or description. There was speculation that she was actually a foreign operative assigned to kill Jock. The theory was that Jock had broken his tibia in the fall, but rather than help him, the woman killed him with the ice axe and shoved him down the mountainside. Nothing was ever proven one way or the other. Jock's name was added to the CIA's wall of honor joining the one hundred plus other names and stars carved into the white Alabama marble. All of them operatives killed in the line of duty.

Jack's mind turned back to the reality of where he was and what he needed to do. He looked around at the room full of strangers. He recognized a few of them from Garrison's wedding. There were another hundred or so he didn't have a clue about, most likely Garrison's co-workers. It was obvious Garrison was well liked. As he surveyed the crowd, he began to wonder, *could Garrison's killer be one of these people? Why would anyone want Garrison dead? Was Garrison's death somehow connected to the death of the OPEC analyst?* Jack began making a list in his mind of people he would need to talk to. The first name that came to mind was Angelina. He decided to wait a day or two before talking to her. He would start first thing tomorrow with some of Garrison's coworkers at Global Oil.

After the assorted funeral hymns and a short sermon, the pastor asked if anyone would care to share something about Garrison. A half dozen people spoke about the good times they had shared with him. None had as many stories to tell as Jack, but he kept quiet. He was focused not on the past, but on the future and finding out who had killed his friend, and why.

When the service finally came to an end, a guest line formed of those offering condolences to Angelina. Jack skipped that part and went out to his rental car where he sat and carefully studied each face as the mourners emerged from the church. *If it's one of you I will find you and you will pay dearly.* A bolt of lightning flashed a few blocks away, followed by loud a clap of thunder that seemed to rock the small church. The storm was getting closer.

Chapter Nine

Global Oil takes up the top five floors of the opulent sixty-four story Williams Tower in the Uptown District of Houston. Located just behind the famous Houston Galleria, the massive oversized chrome and glass monolith looks down on Houston like Goliath looked down on David. The top floor office of Global's CEO Bryson Chandler took up more space than the average three bedroom house. Expensive artwork tastefully adorned every wall and the office furnishings were equally impressive. The centerpiece was a Parnian custom made Cocobolo desk, the kind that cost well into six figures. It was clear that black gold had been good to Chandler. His intercom chimed, "Mr. Chandler, there's a Mr. Wilder here to see you, he says it's about Garrison Shepherd."

"Send him in," Chandler responded, as he stood to greet his visitor.

Chandler's assistant showed Wilder into the lavish office and patiently waited just inside the door.

"Mr. Chandler, thanks for taking the time to see me," Jack said.

Chandler was tall and overbearing, the kind of guy who used his height to intimidate those around him. He was a little heavy, but far from portly. He looked to be in his late fifties, with rapidly graying hair and steely brown eyes. He was wearing a two thousand dollar gray pinstripe Armani suit with a white shirt and a five hundred dollar red silk power tie. His shoes were highly polished cordovan Ferragamos that looked like they just came out of the box.

"Not a problem at all Mr. Wilder, and please, call me Bryson" Chandler said as he shook Jack's hand. " Won't you have a seat?" Chandler gestured toward the sofa. "Would you care for something to drink, coffee, tea, water?"

"Coffee would be great, thanks," Jack said as he sat down on the Corinthian leather couch.

"Two coffees, please, Donna."

"So Mr. Wilder, how can I help you?"

"I suppose you heard about Garrison Shepherd"

"Yes, I understand he worked for us. I was surprised to read about what happened in the paper. Do you know if he had a family"?

"A wife, he was recently married."

Donna discretely came into the room and set a silver tray bearing coffee, cream, sugar and pastries on the coffee table. All contained in the finest Wedgewood Florentine china. Chandler poured two cups of coffee. Jack sipped his as he studied

Chandler's face and eyes. He could usually tell if someone was being truthful by looking at their eyes.

"So, can you tell me how long he worked for you?" Jack asked.

"Actually I can't. We have over five hundred employees here at Global Oil, and regrettably I only know a handful. I simply don't have the time to get out and meet many of them. I'm really not even sure which department he worked in."

"Oh, that's a shame," Jack said. "I was hoping to find out more about what he did here."

"Donna can direct you to our Human Resources Department if you like. I'm sure they can give you much more information than I can."

"Just one more thing," Jack said as he continued to study Chandler's face. "Did you hear about the OPEC analyst who was killed a few days ago?"

"Yes I did, another tragedy. I read about it in the paper. What do you think that's about?"

"I'm not sure, but I understand he also worked for Global Oil at one time and I believe he and Garrison worked together. Were you aware of that?"

"Once again, I'm afraid I can't be of much help. But as I said, I'm sure Human Resources can provide you with lots of information."

The eyes, Jack thought to himself, *the guy is lying.*

"Bryson, thanks very much for your time," Jack said as he stood to leave.

"Not at all, and please don't hesitate to call me if I can be of further assistance. Donna will point you to Human Resources." Chandler pressed the intercom button. "Donna, please show Mr. Wilder the way to HR."

A second later the office door opened and Donna appeared. "Right this way Mr. Wilder." She pulled the door closed behind Jack as he stepped into the outer office. Donna had written something on a slip of paper. "This is the person you want to talk to in Human Resources" she said as she handed Jack the folded slip of paper. "You will find them on the 61st floor."

Jack looked at the slip of paper as he stepped into the elevator and pushed the button for the lobby. He had no intention of going to the HR where he was sure to be further stonewalled by a bunch of HR bozos. He opened the note and read it as the elevator doors closed. There was no name on it. All it said was, *Meet me in front of the Water Wall next door in one hour.*

As soon as Jack left his office, Bryson Chandler took out his cell phone and punched in the Senator's private number. "Why did you have Garrison Shepherd killed?" he demanded. "I just had some guy named Wilder in my office asking all kinds of questions about him." The Senator assured Chandler that they had nothing to do with the killing of Shepherd. Chandler didn't believe him. The last thing he needed was some guy snooping around Global Oil asking about Garrison Shepherd. He had managed to stonewall Wilder, but only for the time being. He could tell Wilder was the kind of guy who wouldn't give up until he found what he was looking for.

Unhappy with the information he got from the Senator, Chandler decided to deal with the matter himself. He called Cisco Lopeno. Cisco was a local thug he'd used in the past to help "persuade" people when they didn't see things his way.

"Cisco, I have a job for you. There's someone I need you to politely ask to leave town."

Chapter 10

Jack killed the next hour at a nearby Starbucks drinking coffee and calling his boss at Langley to give him an update. As he sipped the hot drink he kept asking himself the same questions. *Was there a connection between the Palacios murder and the murder of his friend? What kind of information would they both have had that was worth killing for? Were they even connected at all?* His mind kept going in circles, like a gerbil on an exercise wheel.

Jack walked the four blocks back to the Water Wall, took a seat on a bench facing the giant structure and waited for Donna. The temperature had dropped a couple of degrees and the humidity was climbing. A light wind began to blow smoky gray clouds in from the south. It looked like rain was on the way, a repeat of yesterday's showers.

The horseshoe shaped sixty-four foot high Water Wall was apparently built as a compliment to the sixty-four story Williams Tower next door. It looked like a giant curved washboard with a constant cascade of water falling from both sides. In front of the behemoth fountain, partially obscuring what would otherwise be a great view, stands a kind of proscenium arch structure, totally out of character for the environment. The structure sits on nearly three acres of grass with lines of Texas Live Oaks parading down either side of a huge grassy field.

Two photographers were busy setting up their tripods. Tourists posed for photos in different spots around the park. A young couple stood under one of the high limestone proscenium arches in an embrace while a nearby photographer checked his light meter and made camera adjustments to perfectly capture their romantic hug. A group of Japanese tourists were being herded along by a nervous guide. They walked by at a quick pace, snapping pictures of grass, trees, people, and the huge structure, talking all the while. They were all about the same height and stature. Each had black hair, a bag of tourist goods and a camera hanging from their neck.

Jack turned away from the Japanese tourists just as Donna took a seat on a bench in the shade of one of the Texas Live Oak trees across the way. He got up, walked over and sat beside her. She took a quick nervous glance around, as if to be sure she hadn't been followed. It was clear she wanted their meeting to be private. A long time veteran of Global Oil, Donna Crowley was a slightly overweight, matronly looking woman in her late fifties with dyed red hair in bad need of a touch up. Jack figured she was the type to take new employees and mother them, wanting them to feel free to come to her for advice and counsel. "I believe we may have met at Garrison's wedding," Jack said.

"Indeed we did Mr. Wilder, although I'm surprised you remember me. We met late in the evening, and as I recall, you had quite a lot to drink that night."

"So, what can you tell me about Garrison?" Jack asked, ignoring her comment about his drinking.

"He was a remarkable young man, very dedicated to his work and exceptionally good at what he did. His biggest weakness seemed to be that young wife of his. I honestly don't understand what he saw in her, and I think a lot of his friends felt the same way." She crossed her feet at the ankles, took a deep breath and continued. "He and I would often have lunch or coffee together and he mentioned how he wished things were different with her. He said he was happy, but things weren't quite turning out the way he had hoped. He felt Angelina was too controlling and he was trying to figure out how to deal with it. Even so, I could tell he was still crazy about her."

"Do you know what he was working on at Global? Was it the kind of thing someone would be willing to kill him over?"

"I don't see how it could have been that important. He spent his days looking at charts and other geophysical data. His job was to draw conclusions about where Global should go to look for their next big oil discovery. Honestly, Garrison was so sweet, I can't think of any reason anyone would want to hurt him."

"What about Trini Palacios? I understand he and Garrison worked together at Global before he went to OPEC."

She took another deep breath and shook her head. "Trini was also a great guy. I know he and Garrison were very close when Trini was here. Garrison came here right out of grad school and Trini quickly became a mentor to him. Garrison was truly disappointed when Trini went to OPEC." Something caught her attention and she looked over her shoulder. A little girl chased after a soccer ball that went flying by. "I don't think they saw each other again until Trini and Inez came all the way from Vienna for Garrison's wedding. Honestly, Mr. Wilder, I think the world's gone mad. First Trini was killed by some kind of assassin and then Garrison was killed. Do you think the two murders are related?"

"At this point I don't know what to think," Jack said. "So tell me, why did you slip me the note instead of just asking me to meet with you?"

"Because there have been some strange things going on at Global the last few months. Mr. Chandler has been very secretive for some reason and he has had a few visitors that seemed very different than most people that come to see him." She turned her body toward Jack and looked him in the eye. She pensively bit her lower lip, carefully weighing what she was about to say. "A couple of weeks ago two men showed up without an appointment to see him and they looked like… well – they looked like thugs. There is no other way to describe them. They certainly weren't people from the oil industry. On top of that, I can't understand why Mr. Chandler would have referred you to HR to ask about Garrison. He knew Garrison quite well. Garrison would see him often, sometimes two or three times in one day, to give him research updates. I just have this uneasy feeling that something isn't right."

Donna stood and handed Jack another slip of paper. "Here are the names of a couple more people Garrison worked with that would probably be willing to talk to you. Now I've got to get back before I'm missed. If I think of anything else I will get in touch." She turned and hurried away.

As Donna walked away Jack took a deep breath, tilted his head back and looked up at the darkening Texas sky. He closed his eyes. More questions came. Why was he being stonewalled by Chandler and who were these "thugs" Donna talked about? Why did Donna mention Garrison's problems with Angelina? Why was it that everyone but Garrison could see what a gold digger she was?

Jack called the two Global employees Donna had suggested. No progress there. Both said Garrison was a great guy, well liked by everyone. Couldn't think of any reason anyone would want to hurt him. The bulk of his job had consisted of research on possible new places for Global to look for oil. Both also mentioned their concerns over Garrison's choice of a bride. Neither understood the attraction, yet both agreed he was crazy about the woman. Jack made a mental note to call a friend of his in the Chicago PD. He wanted to know a little more about Angelina's background.

Chapter 11

Ballinger was sitting by the fireplace at the private City Tavern Club in Georgetown drinking his favorite 18 year-old single malt Scotch when the Senator called. The Club was one of Ballinger's favorite getaways and had a colorful history. Originally built in 1796 as an inn and tavern, it was a major hub of civic life. George Washington, Thomas Jefferson and their contemporaries were often seen in the tavern discussing the politics of the day.

Unlike the politics of today, Ballinger imagined the founding fathers had actually cared about the American people, rather than lining their own pockets with cash and pumping up their egos with personal agendas. He didn't think the people he had fought against in Iraq and Afghanistan were actually enemies of the American people. He thought they were the enemies of those greedy Washington bastards, one of whom was his current employer. Ballinger hated the Senator, but loved taking his money. He let the phone ring several times before answering, just to keep him waiting.

"What can I do for you Senator?" he asked as he got up and stepped into a nearby alcove for privacy.

"We have a problem in Houston. It seems an employee of Global Oil named Garrison Shepherd, who used to work with Palacios, has gotten himself killed and that idiot Chandler has his knickers all in a twist. He thinks we did it. He says some guy named

Wilder has been snooping around asking questions about their recently deceased employee. Chandler was happy to go along with the Palacios hit, but now he's starting to panic. I told him we had nothing to do with his guy Shepherd, but I don't think he believed me. He may very well become another liability we have to deal with."

"And this has what to do with me?" Ballinger asked as he took another sip of his Glenlivet. Every time he had a conversation with the Senator he liked him that much less. The condescending bastard treated every one with equal disdain. It was if everyone was put on earth just to do the Senator's bidding. Ballinger had once heard a rumor about the Senator's political tactics. Apparently, early in his political career he was in a dead heat in a congressional race. A week before the election his opponent was killed in a convenient automobile accident. The dead guy still managed twenty-three percent of the total votes. The Senator had won every election since, all the way up to his present office as a member of the U.S. Senate. No one ever asked any questions about the accident.

"I want you to go to Houston and get next to this guy Wilder. Find out what he knows. If he thinks there's a link between Shepherd and Palacios and continues to snoop around, we may have a problem. In the meantime, we'll see how Chandler behaves. If he needs to be dealt with, you can take care of it while you're there."

Ballinger hung up, returned to his seat by the fireplace and ordered another Glenlivet. He needed to think this one through. He was getting in much deeper than he had ever anticipated, plus the fact that he had absolutely no trust in the beloved republican Senator from Texas.

Ballinger pushed himself deeper into the comfortable leather chair... *I wonder just who the hell this Wilder guy is, and what he's up to,* he asked himself. *If I can get close enough to him, there may be a way to turn this thing to my advantage. If not, he may be just another loose end I need to clean up.* The more he thought about it, the more he thought the Senator may fit the "loose end" category as well. He began to feel a little tipsy from too much Glenlivet. Maybe there were no loose ends; maybe it was just the Scotch messing with his mind.

A slightly inebriated and melancholy Ballinger continued to sip his drink. His thoughts turned back in time to the day he made the decision to stop fighting for his country and start fighting for himself. The year was 2008. He had been assigned to a squad in the Kunar Province of Afghanistan near the Pakistan border. He had no sniper duties that day. He had been assigned to work with some Afghan forces when the battle broke out. The first thing he did was call for air cover and reinforcements. Despite repeated calls for air support, it never came. Field commanders deemed it to be too close to civilian populations. He watched, kept firing, and kept calling for support as three fellow marines and 10 Afghan security force members lost their lives, one by one. One brave helicopter pilot defied orders and landed to evacuate one wounded marine who died on the operating table. Lives were lost that day that should have been saved if only the commanders in safe confines of their air conditioned offices had responded to his call. Never again would he depend on anyone for help when things got tough.

Chapter 12

As Jack was driving back to Celeste's apartment, he spotted a huge ugly neon sign of a giant cowboy pointing to Tex's Tavern. *Best booze in Texas, big shots for big shots*, the sign beckoned with an annoying blink from the letter "s" in Texas.

He decided to pull in for a shot or two of Crown Royal Reserve while he contemplated what to do next. He stayed later and drank more than he intended. That's the trouble with really good whiskey. The next one tastes just a little better than the last one. It goes down smooth and then sneaks up on you when you try to get up and walk. Jack made a wobbly trip to the men's room and was on his way out when he decided to have just one more for the road. Bad idea. He downed the last one in three quick swallows and staggered out the door.

It was just after midnight as he stumbled into the nearly empty parking lot. Just as he grabbed the door handle to his rental someone pulled a hood over his head. As he turned and reached up for the hood two giant gorillas grabbed him, one on either side. It was almost as if he were psychic, even with the hood covering his head he somehow knew there was a fist headed for his midsection. He tensed his abs to absorb the blow. He once heard that Harry Houdini would tense his abs and take blows to the stomach to show off what great shape he was in. If it worked for Houdini, is should work for him right? The first punch sounded like a fastball hitting a catcher's mitt and hurt like hell. It knocked the wind out of him. It was then he remembered that Houdini died of a ruptured appendix after taking a hit like that. *Maybe not such a good idea after all.* Still, the Crown Royal was compelling him to offer a few comments to his tormentors.

"Hey Bubba," Jack gasped, "Did anyone ever tell you, you punch like a girl?" Wham! Another fast ball straight across home plate. His knees buckled, but the two giant book ends held him up. "A little better princess, but my grandmother still packs a better punch than you do."

The next one caught him totally off guard, it wasn't to his midsection, it was to his right jaw, followed by another to his midsection. His head vibrated like a jackhammer going into concrete and his stomach felt like it had been put through a wood chipper. The King Kong brothers let go of him and he dropped like a slinky going off the bottom step of a steep staircase.

"You need to stop asking questions about Garrison Shepherd and go back where you came from," one of them said. He heard them start to walk away. He was too weak to move the hood off his head or get up. He could barely breathe, nevertheless, he felt like he needed to have the last word in this little slug fest.

He took in a breath of air and managed to say, "Hey Bubba, you're ugly and your momma dresses you funny." The jackhammer came back again, this time in the form of a size eight cowboy boot. It slammed into his left side like a cannon ball on its way to a battlefield. He was sure he felt a rib crack as it connected, maybe two ribs. From his curled up fetal position, he managed to get a look at the size eight fashion statement through the bottom of the hood. It was a turquoise colored boot with a silver tip on the pointed toe. His mother did dress him funny. Those were the ugliest damn boots he'd ever seen. Boots like that you don't forget. "It's probably just as well," he muttered to no one in particular, "I'm too drunk to drive anyway." His new friends didn't even take the time to say goodbye. They just walked away. Jack closed his left eye, the right was already nearly swollen shut. He held his breath and cautiously rolled onto his back. He pulled the hood off and groaned as he exhaled through the pain and opened his one good eye and looked up at the stars spinning round and round in the dark Texas sky. Somehow he managed to get his cell phone out of his pocket and call Celeste. "Guess what?" he mumbled, as she answered the phone.

Chapter 13

Celeste somehow managed to get Jack up and into the back seat of her Lexus. He sprawled out across the entire seat and moaned again. She was more than a little irritated. Not because she didn't care for Jack, but because she couldn't understand how he had gotten himself into some kind of bar room brawl. She thought he had more sense than that. She didn't care that he moaned in pain each time she hit a bump or pothole on her way back to her apartment. She could tell he was hurt, but knew he'd live.

Back at her apartment, she cleaned him up as best she could, wrapped his chest and ribs with an ace bandage and gave him a bag of frozen peas to hold on his swollen jaw. As he sobered up, he explained what had happened. She believed what he said, but began to wonder where their relationship was headed. If he had a propensity for inviting this kind of violence into his life, was this the kind of life she wanted to share? She knew he was in the CIA and carried a Walter PKJ, or PPJ, or a PBJ or whatever the hell it was he called his damn gun. She had just never given any serious thought to exactly what it was he did for a living or why he carried a gun. She just knew she didn't want to spend her days worrying about him and what kind of danger he was putting himself in. On the other hand, she had to admit, it was kind of a turn on. They spent the night cuddling, knowing anything beyond that was out of the question.

The next morning Celeste took Jack back to Tex's Tavern to retrieve his rental car. They drove most of the way in silence as she was still trying to work out where their relationship was headed and whether or not she wanted to go down that road. Jack was content with the silence and used the time to think about his next course of action. His relationship with Celeste was way down on the list of what he needed to get settled. It was clear he needed to find the guy inside those ugly boots. He also knew he needed to get to Vienna before much more time had passed. He kissed Celeste on the cheek as he carefully and painfully got out of her car and told her he would meet up with her later that evening for dinner.

Jack drove downtown to the Houston Police Department. Given the cozy reception he had experienced by Ugly Boots and the Gorilla brothers, he figured the local PD would probably have had some kind of run in with these bozos in the past. Jack showed the desk sergeant his government ID which allowed him to bypass all the usual paperwork and speak directly to one of the detectives who worked assault crimes.

Detective Stanton Bonham looked like one of those nearly worn out guys who had been on the force forever and was just a day or so away from retirement. He was wearing an inexpensive wrinkled white cotton shirt and a conservative blue and red striped tie. Jack noticed the detective's shoulder holster housed a Smith and Wesson thirty-eight with a well worn grip. Bonham explained they couldn't be of much help without a physical description of the suspect. Ugly turquoise boots with silver tips weren't much of a lead to pursue the low level crime of getting beat up in the parking lot of a bar. It was probably something they had seen hundreds of times and wasn't something that was going to be high on their priority list. Bonham took down Jack's number and promised to call if he found anything out. As Bonham turned to leave Jack said "By the way, can you tell me who the detective is on the Garrison Shepherd case?"

"What's your interest there?" Bonham asked.

"He was a friend, a close friend," Jack replied.

"Follow me," Bonham said as he turned and headed toward the back of the building. Jack followed as they threaded their way through a bull pen filled with cubicles. Bonham pointed to an interview room. "Go in and have a seat. I'll be there in a second." Jack went in and carefully lowered himself into a chair. Even the slightest movement sent pain shooting in all directions in his badly bruised body.

It was a typical police department interview room. A table sat bolted to the floor in the middle of the room. The top of the table had a built in steel bar for attaching handcuffs. The chairs were built to make the interviewee as uncomfortable as possible. A couple of minutes later Bonham came in carrying a slender manila file folder and two cups of coffee. "So tell me about your friend," Bonham said as he handed

Jack one cup and sat down across the table, holding the second cup. "We grew up together in New Mexico. Best friends from first grade through first year of college. I flunked out after a year and Garrison went on to finish up his degree in engineering. He got married less than a year ago. Last time I saw him was at his wedding." Jack took a sip of the stale coffee and stared across the table at Bonham waiting for a response.

"Well, it's actually my case," Bonham said as he opened the folder. "There really isn't a lot to go on. Body was found in a field by a father and son out flying kites. He was shot five times with a nine mil - took four in the middle and upper back and one in the back of the head. There were drag marks in the dirt from the curb that led to a spot about 20 yards into the field where the body ended up. We found a few shoe imprints in between the drag marks, but weren't able to get a size or type on the shoes." Bonham took a sip of his coffee and made a sour face. "Sorry about the coffee," he said "I think it was made sometime last summer."

"Tastes like it for sure," Jack replied as he eased out of the chair and dropped his cup into the trash can in the corner. "So, what else can you tell me?"

"Not much," Bonham said as he pulled a couple of sheets out of the folder and looked over them. "No brass was found anywhere near the body, so he could have been killed anywhere then brought to the dump site. We looked at the wife who said she was out shopping when her husband went for a run. She said he usually ran along the trail by Lions Club Lake at Bane Park." Bonham leaned closer to the file and read a little more. "We had some officers walk the entire path hoping to get lucky and maybe find some brass but didn't. We talked to a few of the regular joggers. One of them saw a dark Mercedes sedan with tinted windows drive by which was a little unusual since there usually aren't many cars in that area. Other than that nothing." Bonham took another sip of coffee, made a face like he'd tasted sour milk. "His wife said she didn't buy anything at the mall, so no receipts to check. We spoke to a few store clerks at the mall where she said she often shopped," he said as he looked at one of the papers in the file. "They recognized her picture, but couldn't remember if she had been in that morning or not. Not a perfect alibi, but certainly a possibility. Funny thing though, she didn't seem too distressed by her husband's death."

"No surprise there," Jack said as he stood to leave. "She was known to be pretty cold hearted. Thanks for your time detective, I would appreciate any information you can find on either case."

Jack decided to go back to Tex's to see if anyone there knew a guy who wore the ugliest boots in Texas. "What happened to you? You look like a horse that's been rode hard and put away wet," the bartender said in slow Texas drawl as Jack took a seat at the bar. "You're the second person to say that to me in the last few days," Jack said "Must be a Texas thing. Actually, I was run over by a Mack truck in your parking lot last night. It was driven by three guys who may have been in here. One of them was wearing a pair of ugly turquoise boots with silver on the toes."

"They wuz in here last night," the bartender said, as he wiped invisible spots off the bar with a towel and leaned a little closer to Jack. "A pair of boots like that you don't forget. I heard one of the other guys call the one with the ugly boots Cisco. I ain't seen any of um in here before. Tough lookin bunch they wuz though, I'll tell you that for sure. Cisco was the smallest of the three. The other two wuz big as gorillas, and looked just about as dumb."

"Gorillas are actually one of the smartest primates," Jack replied, as he laid a ten dollar bill on the bar. "Thanks for your help." As he left, the bartender was scratching his chin and mumbling something about primates being smart. Jack headed back downtown to the PD.

Detective Bonham had checked out for the rest of the day, so he gave the sergeant Cisco's name, told him about the ugly boots and asked him to pass the information along to the detective. The sergeant took Jack's number and said someone would be in touch.

Jack left the Houston PD thinking it was time to go to Vienna to see what he could find out. He called the CIA travel group on his way back to Celeste's apartment. They booked him on a commercial airline leaving Houston at five a.m. the next day. Flying commercially made carrying his Glock and its associated hardware a little more complex than flying on a military aircraft. He drove to the Houston Regional Office of the Office of Foreign Missions. Using his CIA credentials, he picked up an empty diplomatic pouch. Diplomatic pouches are immune from screening and searching at airports and customs. It was once rumored that Winston Churchill used the diplomatic pouch to get his Cuban cigars delivered during World War II. Jack's weapons and ammunition fit nicely in the discreet leather pouch he was given.

Chapter 14

Ballinger's flight from DC on Southwest Airlines arrived at Houston's Hobby Field a little past three thirty in the afternoon. He made his way through the terminal and out to the Hertz gold customer rental booth to pick up his waiting car. The temperature outside was eighty-five degrees and the high humidity added more misery to the Texas weather.

Ballinger hated Texas. He hated everything about it. He hated the way they talked with their stupid Texas drawls. He hated their politics and their politicians, with the exception of Ann Richards. Now there was a woman with a head on her shoulders. The only other good thing that ever came out of Texas was Molly Ivins. She once wrote that there were more people killed by guns in Texas than were killed in automobile accidents. She said the Texas legislature wasted no time passing a law to deal with the issue - they raised the speed limit. You gotta love the simplicity of Texas logic.

Ballinger drove his rented Cadillac through the lot and out the exit. He picked up Interstate forty-five north for a few miles, then jumped onto the Southwest Freeway. Traffic was starting to bunch up, like trout going through a garden hose. Just one more Texas aggravation. He drove past a strip mall with a sign out front, "Donuts, Guns and Daycare." Where else but Texas? He took the West Loop exit, got off on Post Oak Boulevard and parked a block away from the Williams Tower. The Senator had sent him to pay Bryson Chandler a visit.

It was just after five when Ballinger arrived. All the administrative staff had left for the day, but Ballinger knew Chandler would still be in. He walked into Chandler's office, sat on one of the expensive leather couches and put his feet up on the eight thousand dollar coffee table. He didn't like Chandler. He thought of him as a mousy little weasel and liked to intimidate the guy every chance he could. He hated the way Chandler flaunted his wealth, knowing that he made it on the backs of honest, hardworking men and women in the oil fields. Those poor chumps who worked hard to make ends meet, while guys like Chandler lied, cheated and stole their way to the top. Chandler gave Ballinger a disgruntled look, then smiled and said, "Ballinger my old friend, what brings you to town? Care for a drink? As I recall you're a Scotch man, right?"

"Glenlivet on the rocks," Ballinger replied, as he shifted his feet on the expensive table. "I heard you had a visit from a guy named Jack Wilder asking about the death of one of your employees, Garrison Shepherd."

"That's right. The guy came in here asking all kinds of questions. He knows that Shepherd and Palacios worked together here at Global Oil a few years back. I understand why we needed to get rid of Palacios, but I don't understand why someone ordered a hit on one of my employees."

"We had nothing to do with that, I thought the Senator made that clear."

Chandler glanced nervously around the room as if he were looking for someone, anyone, to be on his side as he argued with Ballinger.

"Maybe so, but the Senator isn't known for always being truthful when it comes to some of his more unusual business dealings. Besides, it's no longer an issue, I took care of it."

"Oh and just how did you take care of it?" Ballinger asked, as he put his feet on the floor and set his glass on the coffee table, ignoring the coaster Chandler had set out when he handed him the expensive Scotch.

"I called a guy I know, Cisco. He takes care of problems for me once in awhile. Problems like when I want somebody to go away. Cisco has a way of persuading them to leave. He took care of Wilder. I don't think the guy will be asking anymore questions."

"You don't think? You see Chandler, that's the problem with you, you don't think. Thinking is not what you are paid to do. Thinking is for someone higher up the food chain, someone like the Senator." Ballinger picked up his drink and took the last swallow of Scotch. As he stood to leave he said "And one more thing... you pull another stupid stunt like that and I'll personally drag your sorry ass up to the roof of this Texas phallic symbol we're standing in and throw you over the side. Got it? Now tell me, where can I find this Cisco guy."

Chandler's hand was shaking as he wrote down the address for Cisco's apartment and handed it to Ballinger. Chandler began to hyperventilate. His heart pounded in his chest like it was going to explode. He knew Ballinger well enough to know that he wasn't joking about throwing him off the roof. He couldn't help but wonder if his forthcoming trip to the Senator's ranch might be a one way trip. After Ballinger left, Chandler poured himself a stiff drink, something he had taken to doing more and more frequently for the past year. Each time, he found it harder to stop.

Chapter 15

Cisco Lopeno opened the door to his apartment and reached for the light switch. Just as he flipped the switch he felt a loud crack and sudden pain as something hit the back of his head. The lights went out. When he woke up he was sitting on the floor of his apartment leaning against his couch. He had a splitting headache. His feet and mouth were bound with duct tape and his wrists were locked together with flex cuffs. He looked up at the muscular stranger sitting in the chair in front of him. The guy was holding a nine millimeter Beretta in one hand and it was pointed directly at Cisco's head. Cisco had a sense that his headache could become fatal any second.

"Hello Cisco, my name is Mr. Smith," Ballinger said. "I thought perhaps you and I should get to know each other a little. I believe we have a good friend in common, Mr. Bryson Chandler." Cisco took in a deep breath through his nose and stared at the stranger, wondering what he wanted. "Here's what we're going to do," Ballinger said as he grabbed hold of Cisco's little finger on his bound left hand. "I'm going to ask you some questions and for every lie you tell me I'm going to break one of your fingers." With his free hand, Ballinger pulled the tape off Cisco's mouth.

"Now, tell me about Jack Wilder."

"I don't know any Jack Wilder."

Ballinger gave a quick jerk with his hand and the top half of Cisco's little finger snapped to a ninety degree angle. Cisco gritted his teeth and screamed as Ballinger took hold of Cisco's ring finger. "Let's try that again," Ballinger said.

"Okay, okay," Cisco said as he grimaced, hoping he wouldn't find himself with another broken finger. "I do know this Wilder dude, Chandler hired me and the guys to rough him up a little and tell him to stop asking questions and leave town."

"How did you find him?"

"Chandler's security guy showed me the video of him leaving the building. We didn't even have to look for the guy. When we left the building we saw him talking to Chandler's secretary or whatever she is. He was next door at that Water Wall place, you know, the place with the water, like on the wall and everything? Anyway, we followed him to a bar and worked him over and left him in the parking lot. A little while later this good looking blonde lady in a silver Lexus came to pick him up. She put him in the car and they drove off. We followed them to her place to make sure they wasn't going to the cops. After that we took off."

"Good job Cisco, now tell me where this good looking lady lives," Ballinger said as he stood to leave. Cisco was quick to provide directions for him. Ballinger opened the door, turned and said, "I'll be seeing you around my friend, and one more thing…don't be doing any more work for Bryson Chandler. If I find out you are doing anything for him, I'll be back for another little visit. Trust me, you don't want that to happen. I don't leave people beat up in parking lots, I leave them in the morgue." Cisco took a deep breath. He really, really didn't want this Mr. Smith coming back, ever.

Chapter 16

Celeste got out of bed just after six the next morning. As she got ready for work she vaguely remembered Jack kissing her goodbye around four as he left for the airport. He said something about going to Vienna and being back in a few days.

Ballinger sat patiently in his car across the street from Celeste's apartment building. The structure was a modern six story, higher end complex located just off West Dallas Street close to the Museum District and San Felipe Park. The place looked more like a four star hotel than an apartment building. It appeared to have all the amenities required by young professionals on their way up. There was a pool, a sauna, tennis courts, and of course the obligatory on-site workout facility. Celeste's apartment was on the first floor with a large covered porch adjacent to a short stairway that led to a nicely landscaped courtyard. The courtyard was bordered by a large parking area.

Ballinger recognized her right away as she came out of her apartment and turned to lock the door. Cisco had done a good job of describing her and he was right, she was very good looking. She had her blonde hair pulled back in a pony tail and was wearing a pair of black slacks and a yellow blouse. The yellow highlighted her delicate features and blonde hair. Jack Wilder had chosen well. As a rule Ballinger didn't harm women. He had scared plenty of them in his career, usually by threatening to do something to their husbands or boyfriends if they were unwilling to cooperate. In the end, they always did and none of them were ever harmed. He couldn't say the same for husbands and boyfriends.

Ballinger watched as she got into her silver Lexus. He started his rented Cadillac, checked his side mirror, made a U turn and pulled in behind her as she drove past. He stayed a few cars back. She had no idea she was being followed. A few blocks later she pulled into the parking lot of a Starbucks and slipped into a space far from the door. Ballinger pulled into the empty space beside her. They both got out of their cars at the same time.

"Good morning," he said. "Getting your caffeine fix before heading into work eh?"

"Yup, can't live without it," she said.

He walked next to her as they made their way across the parking lot to the entrance.

"Great weather we're having isn't it?" he said.

"Yeah, not bad for this time of year."

He held the door for her and followed her in as they both took a place in the long line to order.

As they reached the head of the slow moving line they overheard the guy in front of them arguing with the cashier. "But it's just plain stupid," he was saying.

"If I buy three drinks I should get three reward stars, not just one. It makes no sense at all." The cashier smiled, she'd heard the same argument hundreds of times, and she always gave the same answer. "Please visit the Starbucks' website and click on the suggestion box to let them know how you feel." The guy just shrugged, picked up his three drinks and headed for the nearest table.

"So do you live around here?' Ballinger said, as the line slowly inched forward.

"A few blocks away. How about you?"

"Actually a few hundred miles away, Baltimore. I'm here on business, have to meet with some pesky oil people downtown."

"Well, I guess oil does make the world go round," she replied as she stepped up to the counter and ordered a Grande Skinny Vanilla Latte. "Maybe you can talk them into lowering gas prices," she said. "It's becoming insane, they way they keep rising."

"Sorry, can't help you with that. I'm a contracts guy, spend my time dotting i's and crossing t's.

"Oh well, it is what it is I guess. Nice talking to you," she said, as she paid and turned to walk away.

"Good talking to you too," Ballinger replied. "Maybe I'll see you here again. I'm in town for a few more days."

Ballinger ordered a tall black coffee and sat down at a table by the window and watched her get into her car and drive away. He sat awhile longer, finishing his coffee and watching people come and go. He eavesdropped on conversations, businessmen, talking about closing deals and soccer moms talking about schools and kids. A few people were frantically punching keys on laptops. Probably college students finishing up papers due later that day or maybe an author working on his next great novel. He took the last sip of his coffee and headed for the door.

Traffic was still light, and the temperature and humidity were rising as Ballinger made the short drive back to Celeste's apartment. *Another warm, humid Houston day, damn I hate this town.* He parked under a huge Live Oak and patiently watched Celeste's front door and the surrounding area. He wanted to make sure there were no nosey neighbors lurking about. He also wanted to get a feel for whether anyone else may be in the apartment.

Thirty minutes later Ballinger walked up to the door and rang the bell. No one answered. He had the lock picked in less than 20 seconds. He put on a pair of gloves, and then screwed the silencer onto the barrel of his Glock 17 as he stepped through the door. He turned slightly and listened for any sound or movement in the apartment. He unlatched the sliding glass door off the kitchen that led to a small, gated patio that opened into another courtyard. Breaking and entering 101, always give yourself more than one way out.

Satisfied he was alone, he began a more thorough search without knowing exactly what he was looking for. He needed to know more about Celeste and Jack, or more specifically where Jack was and what he was up to. He started his search in the bathroom off the master bedroom. Typical lady items were neatly clustered on the vanity, hand lotion, skin care products, cotton balls, birth control pills and so on. The bathroom was a pale maroon with windows trimmed in white. Gray rugs, bath mat and towels accented the maroon and white. Ballinger looked in the medicine cabinet and found nothing stronger than aspirin. He meticulously put each item back exactly as he found it, as he methodically worked his way around the room.

He continued his search room by room. The master bedroom had a neatly made queen size bed with a light gray duvet and dark gray pillow covers. He looked in each of the bedside tables and found nothing out of the ordinary. He looked under the bed, nothing there other than dust. He carefully opened each drawer of her dresser and looked under all her clothing, no sign of a diary. Just a lot of classy underwear that looked like it came out of a Victoria Secret catalog. He wondered how much of it Jack had seen on her trim body.

There were the usual assortment of family pictures and mementos on top of the dresser. Pictures of what were probably her parents, her college graduation and a picture of two older people, probably grandparents. Another frame held a picture of Celeste at about age 10 in a soccer uniform. The last one was of Celeste standing between two guys. One looked older, the other younger, probably brothers.

He found her laptop in the spare bedroom and booted it up, lots of emails back and forth between various friends, a spreadsheet containing all of her household expenses and a couple of letters to out of town relatives. The emails were mostly a lot of girl talk about Jack Wilder and what a hunk he was. There was also a mention of how great the hunk was in bed. Ballinger had hoped to find some sign of Jack in the apartment, but there was none. *Where had lover boy gone?*

After browsing through the kitchen and living room, Ballinger locked the front door from inside and left the apartment through the sliding glass door to the patio. He walked back to his car and called the Senator to report his findings. No Jack Wilder to be found today.

Chapter 17

After a 12 hour flight on Lufthansa Airlines with layovers in Chicago and Munich, Jack arrived in Vienna just past midnight. As he expected, getting through customs was a breeze. The diplomatic pouch always gets its carrier preferential treatment at airports. He took a cab to the Hotel Vienna just around the corner from the Johann Strauss Museum. He paid the driver, checked in at the front desk and took the elevator up to his room on the fourth floor. He kicked off his shoes and sat on the bed.

Just as he got comfortable there was a knock at his door. He opened the pouch, removed his Walther PPK and held it down at his side as he looked through the peep hole in the door. He saw a short, thin wiry looking fellow with a heavy moustache holding his Interpol credentials up where they could be seen through the peep hole. He was accompanied by two much taller and heavier gentlemen standing on either side of him. Somehow Jack found the sight a little comical. The short guy in the middle reminded him of Inspector Clouseau from the Pink Panther movies. Jack tucked the PPK in the back of his waist band, slipped on his jacket and opened the door.

"Good morning gentlemen, what can I do for you?" Jack asked, as he opened the door. "You are Mr. Wilder, Mr. Jack Wilder, yes?" said the small fellow as they all rudely walked into the room without waiting for an invitation. "I am Special Agent

Aledo Boerne of the International Criminal Police Organization. You will come with us please."

"Guys, I'm kinda tired, I just spent 12 hours riding on airplanes. Can't we do this tomorrow?"

"We cannot," Boerne replied. "We have been sent to pick you up. The Staatspolizei are waiting to speak with you now." Jack was very familiar with the Staatspolizei. Commonly known as Stapo, they were the secret service branch of the Austrian Federal Police. Their purview was primarily counter terrorism and counter intelligence. He wondered what they wanted with him.

It was a short ride to Stapo headquarters and Jack was glad. They were all crammed into an old beat up Renault. The small guy drove while Jack sat in the back seat sandwiched between big and bigger. He was frisked, relieved of his Walther PPK and taken into a drab gray room with poor lighting and no outside windows. The last coat of paint the room had seen was probably slapped on somewhere around the time of the Spanish Inquisition. Four well worn chairs sat in the gloomy room around an ugly green table. Jack parked himself at the end of the table with a clear view of the door and tried to get comfortable.

A half hour later, a tall muscular guy about Jack's height and build came into the room carrying a cup of coffee in each hand and a file tucked under his arm. Jack recognized the guy immediately. He was Evant Darrouzett. Jack had worked with him on a six month operation in Paris three years earlier. They had monitored a suspected terrorist cell made up of four guys from Yemen. The terrorists had planned to plant bombs to go off simultaneously at the Eiffel Tower, the Louvre, the Hotel de Crillon and the Paris subway. Part of the operation had gone sour and Evant was nearly killed by one of the terrorists.

The terrorists made their move a day early and Jack and Evant had to go in before things were in place. Evant had gone into the terrorist apartment ahead of Jack and didn't notice the small room off the entry hall to the apartment and rushed right past it. One of the terrorists stepped out of it and was about to shoot Evant in the back when Jack came into the entryway. Jack got his shot off first. Evant killed two others as they headed for the fire escape and turned to fire at him. The fourth one made it down the fire escape and was hit and killed by a truck as he ran across Rue de Rivoli in rush hour traffic. Apparently at terrorist school they don't cover childhood mandates like looking both ways before crossing the street.

Darrouzette set the coffees and the file on the table and the two of them hugged each other like long lost brothers.

"Ev," Jack said, "it's good to see you. But would you mind telling me just why in the hell I'm here?"

"Standard procedure, Jack. Interpol told us your group was taking the lead on this OPEC killing, but when you showed up unannounced we needed to bring you in. We need to know what your plan of action is. After all, we can't have you running amok scaring our citizens and making waves. This whole OPEC thing is a sensitive issue."

Jack took a sip of his coffee and looked around the room before turning back to Evant. The only thing he had on his agenda was to talk to Palacios' widow and some of the people he'd worked with at OPEC. He didn't know where he would go from there.

"Great place you have here," Jack said, "but I would recommend you fire your interior decorator and maybe think about getting some new furniture."

"I'll give that some thought," Evant replied, "but don't change the subject. What are your plans?"

"Not much really, first talk to the widow, then some of Palacios' colleagues at OPEC. I will have to wait and see where that leads me. What can you tell me about the assassination?"

"Not a whole lot," Evant said as he opened the file, turned it around and pushed it across the table. "Based on the trajectory of the bullet we were able to pinpoint where the shot came from. It was fired from the top of the Zurich building about eight blocks away. We found an American made Barrett M82A1 sniper rifle in a dumpster behind the building." Evant blew on his coffee and took a slow sip. "We also recovered several nine mil slugs from a few buildings and cars in the area just outside the Zurich building. We think the killer wanted to create a diversion to help cover his exit. Someone also pulled one of the fire alarms in the Zurich building to further add to the chaos." Evant took another sip of his coffee. "No one in the Zurich building saw anyone pull any of the alarms and of course no prints to be found anywhere. This guy is a pro, no doubt about it."

They both finished the last of their coffee and agreed to keep in touch and share any new information. Clouseau, sans big and bigger, drove Jack back to his hotel.

Chapter 18

The weather had cooled and a light rain was falling at just after seven a.m. when Jack rang the bell of the luxury OPEC apartment occupied by the widow Palacios and her two children. Inez Palacios answered the door in her casual morning sweat pants, an oversized sweatshirt and no make-up. Her long dark hair was pulled back in a makeshift pony tail. She was even more beautiful than Jack remembered. As he looked at her, he also saw a tremendous sadness in her dark brown eyes. She was clearly struggling to put her life back together.

The smell of bacon frying had followed her to the door. Eleven year old Daisetta and her seven year old brother Pantego were busy setting the table in the kitchen behind her. Pantego had inherited his father's pointed nose. He had dark eyes, a mop of unruly black hair and looked to be a little overweight for his age. Daisetta clearly took after her mother. She was a petite young lady with long dark hair, a smooth creamy complexion and the facial features of a young model. Both kids had come to the door when they heard the ringing of the doorbell. Inez gave them a stern look and pointed to the hallway. They made a quick retreat to their bedrooms.

Pantego's voice filled the long ornate hallway as he hurried to his room to finish getting dressed. "Mom, have you seen my Nikes?" instantly followed by Daisetta's bellowing, "Look under your bed, dummy."

"Jack, come in," Inez said as she opened the door. "It's nice to see you again. May I offer you some coffee?"

"That would be great," he replied as he stepped into the entryway, removed his coat, and hung it on the elaborate hall tree by the door. He followed her into the kitchen. There was a small vase of fresh flowers in the middle of the table. The kid's plates were set opposite the floral arrangement. A glass of freshly squeezed orange juice sat by each plate, waiting to be gulped down by ravenous young appetites.

"Have a seat at the table. I'll have these kids fed and out of here in a few minutes then we can talk," Inez said as she poured his coffee.

Jack sipped his coffee taking in the sights and sounds of the fatherless Palacios family. Daisetta and Pantego came back in neatly dressed and carrying book bags. Daisetta took a seat by Jack. Pantego gulped down his juice, picked up his plate, moved to the opposite side of the table and sat on Jack's other side. Jack looked down at each young face. For a brief instant he thought of Celeste, picturing himself with her and a couple of kids. One big happy family sitting down to breakfast. *Hmm, ain't never gonna happen,* he thought to himself.

"Who are you?" the precocious Pantego asked.

"I'm a friend of your mother's."

"Are you gonna help us find out who killed my dad?"

Jack's heart sank. He couldn't begin to imagine how difficult it must be for these kids to have lost their father. "Well, I'm certainly going to try."

A quick five minutes later, both kids had inhaled their breakfast and were out the door and on their way downstairs to meet the limousine that would take them to school. Thankfully, Inez was still able to enjoy a few of the OPEC perks afforded her late husband. The limousine school bus and the OPEC apartment came with Trini's job.

"Inez, I'm so sorry for your loss," Jack said, as an air of silence filled the room.

"And yours as well," she replied. "I heard about Garrison, I know you were best of friends. Do you think his death was related to Trini's?"

"At this point, it's too early to tell, but it certainly is a strange coincidence. Trini and Garrison certainly had a lot in common. Do you have any idea what Trini may have been working on at OPEC?" Jack took another sip of coffee and looked again at Inez's sad eyes. They had both lost someone they loved and he was now more determined than ever to get to the bottom of it.

"I really don't," Inez said. "But I do know he was bothered by something. He seemed very distant distracted the week before he died. When I asked him what it was about he just said it was some work issues he was dealing with."

She picked up the kids' dishes, carried them to the sink and poured herself another cup of coffee. She sat back down, let out a heavy sigh and stared at her coffee cup as she gently rolled it back and forth between the palms of her hands. "Jack, I do know that he tried to get in touch with Garrison but was unable to reach him. He left a package on his desk and asked me to send it to Garrison. But with all that happened, I never got around to doing it and now with Garrison gone too…." Jack could see she was fighting to keep her tears in check.

Inez stood and turned away to hide the tears as she went to Trini's study and retrieved the package from his desk. She returned to the table and sat the parcel down next to Jack's coffee cup. She sat back down and once again turned her focus to the warm cup she held in her hands. "Thanks," Jack said, "I will have some people look at it. Is there anything else you can think of that may help us solve this thing?"

Inez furrowed her brow and thought for a second. "There is a guy Trini worked with that he thought very highly of, his name is Damon Escobares. He was always comparing him to Garrison and telling me that Damon was nearly as smart as Garrison." He may be able to help you with whatever it was Trini was working on."

They spent another hour reminiscing about Garrison and Trini, telling each other stories about the good times they had shared with their loved ones. Finally, Jack thanked her for the coffee and stood to leave. She gave him a hug as he picked up the package and headed for the door. Inez followed him into the hall and held the bundle while Jack shrugged into his coat. He put a hand on each of her shoulders and looked into her dark eyes. He took his right hand and brushed a wisp of hair out of her face. "Inez, I swear to you, I will find out who did this and they will pay." She gently closed the door behind him as he left. He could hear her quietly sobbing as he walked away.

The rain had stopped and the sun was trying to peek out from behind the clouds as Jack left the building. He took out his cell phone and called Damon Escobares and arranged to meet him for lunch. Then he called Barry Godley, a computer geek friend of his at Langley. Barry got his PhD in Computer Science at Princeton when he was 19. Anytime Jack had a conversation with him, he only understood about half of what the guy said. Around the office Godley was known as Barry the Wonder Boy. He told the whiz kid to expect a package of data on some kind of oil usage analysis and to get back to him with what it was all about. He went back to his hotel and had the concierge Fed Ex the package to Barry.

Chapter 19

Hamilton Kingsbury III was a man who always got his way. He was a short man, only five-seven, with all the traits of a Napoleon complex. He was overly aggressive and domineering at every turn. He had a quick temper and would fly into a rage at the slightest provocation. His face was narrow with a slightly hooked nose and small, beady eyes. He wore custom tailored suits, perfectly cut for his small frame. Those few souls brave enough to stand up to him were quickly destroyed and left in ruins. There was a perverse joy the Senator seemed to take in the ruination of those who would oppose him. To him it was a game, one that he always won.

Hamilton was an only child, born rich and raised even richer. A gifted academic, he saw education as a minor inconvenience. He attended Exeter Academy prep school in New Hampshire before going to Yale for his undergraduate degree and his MBA. While at Exeter he got into an argument with a fellow student over a girl. After an anonymous call to the dean, a small quantity of marijuana was found under the student's bed and he was expelled. Word quickly spread - don't cross Hamilton Kingsbury III.

Hamilton's family wealth came from oil money. His grandfather was a wildcat oil man who happened to find the right strike at the right time. The money began to grow as it flowed down through the generations. Hamilton's father had somewhat of a Midas touch and parlayed his inheritance into an even bigger fortune. Hamilton was the shrewdest and most ruthless of all the Kingsbury men. After his father died he sold the entire lot to the British Energy Corporation for just over three and a half billion in cash and stock. A year after his father died he put his mother in an expensive nursing home in upstate New York where she remained until her death 10 years later. During that time she only received one visit from her only child, and that was because he needed a signature. Other than that, never a card or a letter.

Hamilton used a portion of his fortune to buy controlling interest in Global Oil. With his power and connections he had Bryson Chandler installed as the CEO of Global. He then set up a series of shell investment companies and set about buying a controlling interest in a variety of rapidly growing oil companies. While the various CEOs ran their companies, they all knew that it was Hamilton holding the purse strings; it was Hamilton who had the power to move their companies in any direction he chose. He personally chose each member of every company's board of directors.

Although he was obscenely wealthy, the thing he coveted the most was power, power and control. Soon after becoming a billionaire, he set his sights on Washington DC. What better place to find the ultimate power and control than in the U.S. Senate. After two terms as a Texas congressman, he entered the Senate race. He easily outspent and out maneuvered his opponent. He spent over a million alone on the covert operations he needed to destroy his opponent. By the time the election came around his opponent had been photographed with a prostitute, video-taped taking bribes and pulled over by a policeman who conveniently found a small quantity of marijuana in his car.

Hamilton was now in the third year of his second Senate term. He had to call in several political favors and spent another million or so in outright bribes to fellow politicians to get himself appointed as the chair of the Committee on Energy and Natural resources. His committee was made up of four subcommittees: Energy, National Parks, Public Lands and Water and Power. He only cared about, and kept his finger on the pulse of one, Energy. Among other things, this elite group had oversight for oil and natural gas regulation, refinery policies, coal conversion, utility policy and strategic petroleum reserves. There were 17 members of that sub-committee and 10 of them were solidly in his pocket. Despite the committee overseeing oil and refinery policies they weren't privy to what Hamilton knew.

During the next year, Kingsbury planned to expand his power base, increase his already huge fortune and begin his march to the White House. He had already begun to set things in motion for his Presidential campaign. His plan was nearly ruined when an OPEC analyst came across the fictitious oil shortage he and his OPEC friends had created and was about to tell the world about it. He had received a call from an OPEC insider who told him about Palacios' discovery. He knew it was a matter of time before Palacios would say something and things would begin to unravel. If Palacios had started making waves and talking about what he'd found, the Senator's plans would have been ruined. There would have been investigations by every federal agency imaginable. There would have been senate hearings, subpoenas issued, sworn testimony, legal wrangling and in all likelihood the Federal Government would have taken control of all the U.S. oil holdings until things could be sorted out. And perhaps most devastating would have been the panic selling of oil stocks, oil stocks that accounted for a large portion of his fortune.

No, Hamilton Kingsbury III wasn't about to let all that happen. The announcement of the fictitious shortage had to be made when he was gearing up to run for President. It was carefully planned that he would be the one to "discover" the alleged oil shortage and ride in on his white horse to save the world from the evils of greedy oil companies. By exposing the shortage, he would endear himself to the American public. The same public who would see it in their hearts to vote him into the presidency. Although Ballinger was expensive, the Senator felt that silencing the OPEC analyst had been money well spent.

Chapter 20

Damon Escobares was a handsome young man with the characteristic dark hair and olive skin attributed to many men from Venezuela. He had attended Simon Bolivar University which was Trini's alma mater. Trini had, in fact, helped Damon land his analyst job at OPEC. The two had worked together for two years. Damon was a protégé to Trini in the OPEC organization much like Garrison Shepherd had been when Trini worked at Global Oil.

Damon was sitting at a table near the bar at Fabios Italian restaurant. Located on Tuchlauben, Fabios is a short walk from the OPEC building making it a convenient place to meet. The front of the restaurant was a mosaic of giant windows that opened to a sidewalk for outdoor dining when weather permitted. The main dining area had booths with high backs, hardwood floors and wooden accents everywhere you looked. A cozy, dimly lit bar took up one end of the restaurant adjacent to the cozy booths. The bar itself was made of some kind of limestone with tiny lights inlaid to add a touch of intimacy. The black ceiling was dotted with small lights to further add to the elegant ambience.

The open windows gave Jack a clear view of Damon as he stood across Tuchlauben and watched the waiter seat the young man in one of the high backed booths near the bar. The young OPEC analyst was easy to spot, wearing the red shirt and black slacks he'd described to Jack on the phone. Damon glanced nervously around as he waited for Jack to arrive. Having worked for many years as a CIA field operative both following people and being followed, Jack could easily tell if something was amiss in the crowded street and restaurant.

Satisfied that Damon hadn't been followed, Jack crossed the street and went into the crowded restaurant to join the nervous young analyst. "Damon, nice to meet you, thanks for coming to see me on such short notice," Jack said as he reached out to shake hands with Damon.

"Nice to meet you as well," Damon replied as he shook Jack's hand. The two of them sat down and a waiter instantly appeared, poured two glasses of water and handed each of them a menu. Damon scanned his briefly, gave the waiter his order and anxiously waited for Jack to start the conversation. Jack asked for coffee and gave the waiter the rest of his order without looking at the menu.

After a few minutes of small talk about Damon's education and background Jack took a sip of coffee and said "So Damon, what can you tell me about Trini? Do you have any idea what he was working on before he was killed?" The waiter delivered their lunch orders just as Jack finished the question. Pasta Primavera for Damon and a steak for Jack, rare. Damon waited for the waiter to leave before answering.

"I can't say for sure but I believe it may have had something to do with the oil shortage. The last few weeks he was very secretive about what he was doing. He was unusually obsessed about oil production being reduced by several of the OPEC countries." Damon took a sip from his glass of water and leaned in a little closer. "He once said that some of the numbers coming in didn't make any sense, like they were bogus numbers."

"I'm not sure I follow," Jack said. "Are you telling me he thought the oil shortage wasn't real?"

"I can't say for sure, I'm just saying it looks like that may have been what he was working on. He recently asked me to run some calculations on the average number of barrels produced by an oil well before it runs dry. I think he was looking at when all the existing wells, or at least the major wells, normally run out of crude." Damon took another sip of his water and glanced around the room again. He wanted to make sure no one was listening. "I really don't understand what he was looking at. Up until about six months ago the numbers all said there was enough crude in the ground and in reserves to last another hundred years or so." Escobar took another bite of his pasta and waited for Jack's next question.

"Aside from you, what about other people Trini worked with?" Jack asked. "Did you get a sense that there was any kind of friction between Trini and any of the other employees?"

"Oh, he could be obstinate and aloof sometimes" Escobar replied, "but overall he got along quite well with everybody. I never heard anyone say an unkind word about him."

"Who else might have known what he was working on?"

"Probably no one," Escobar responded. "I was assigned to work with him on anything he needed. I never saw anyone else ask or offer anything that seemed pertinent to what was going on."

"What about the people he used to work with at Global oil? Did he ever say anything about any of them or any problems he may have had while he worked there?"

"No, he hardly ever spoke about his days at Global. When he did, he always talked about what a great place it was to work and how he missed a lot of his old colleagues."

After a lengthy discussion about oil extraction technology, which Jack found boring and hard to follow, and Damon's job function at OPEC, the young analyst looked at his watch. "I've got to get back," he said as he took the last bite of his pasta. They both stood. Jack thanked him, gave him a card and asked him to call if he remembered or found out anything else. Jack watched him leave and sat back down to finish his coffee.

Jack turned his attention to the man sitting alone two tables over. The guy had a thick black moustache, olive skin and black hair. All during lunch every time Jack looked up at the mirror behind the bar he could see the man staring at him and Damon in the mirror as if he was trying to understand what they were saying. Jack paid the tab and left.

He casually strolled down Tuchlauben Avenue, stopping occasionally pretending to look into the windows. As he suspected, the guy with the moustache was following him. Jack swore at himself for not noticing the stranger when he was watching the restaurant from across the street. Jack made a quick turn to the right into an alley and jogged fifty feet or so before ducking into a doorway. After about a minute, moustache man came into view. Jack stepped out of the doorway, grabbed the guy by the lapels and slammed him against the wall.

"Who are you and why are you following me?" Jack demanded as he slammed the guy against the wall a second time.

"I am Nurillo Muniz from Interpol," the wide eyed stranger sputtered as he struggled nervously to reach into his outer coat pocket for ID.

"They told me to follow you and report back. They want to know where you go and who you meet with," the man said as he showed Jack his black and gold Interpol ID and rubbed the back of his head with his free hand.

"You go back and tell them who I meet with is none of their damn business and if I catch you following me again a lot more than the back of your head will hurt next time." Jack grabbed the stranger by the shoulders, turned him towards the entry to the alley and gave him a shove and a kick in the seat of his pants. The man stumbled, regained his foot hold and ran out of the alley.

Jack pulled out his cell phone and dialed Evant Darrouzett.

"Evant, it's Jack. I thought we had a deal. I was going to let you know if I found out anything. You didn't have to send someone to follow me."

"What the hell are you talking about Jack? We don't have anyone following you."

"Well some little weasel from Interpol and I just had a short conversation in an alley off Tuchlauben. Clumsy type as it turned out - somehow he slipped and smacked his head against the wall while we were having our conversation."

"Jack, I work for Stapo, not Interpol, but they would not have had you followed without keeping us in the loop. Did he happen to give you his name before he "slipped" and hit his head?"

"Matter of fact he did. Said he was Nurillo Muniz, showed me his Interpol ID."

"Well, here's the thing Jack, I know all the Interpol guys in Vienna and there is no Nurillo Muniz in their organization. I'll ask around and see if I can figure out what's going on. In the meantime, were you able to make any headway with the OPEC people?"

"Not much, the guy I met with said Palacios seemed obsessed with a theory that this whole oil shortage is totally bogus."

"Hmm, that's interesting. I'll do some checking from that angle as well. Stay in touch and watch your back Jack."

Chapter 21

The Kingsbury ranch is a 20,000 acre working cattle ranch located on top of a high mountain plateau at the end of a steep windy two lane road in Northern Montana. The place is staffed and run by no less than thirty people at any one time. Half of those are the Senator's security detail. Kingsbury had no idea whether or not the ranch made any money in the volatile cattle market, and he really didn't care. What he did care about was having a comfortable secure place to conduct business.

The main lodge of the ranch sat in its own secure compound. In addition to optic sensors around the circumference of the property, nightly patrols by armed guards accompanied by well trained Rottweilers were a frequent occurrence. The main entry to the compound was through an iron gate just over a half mile from the lodge. Just outside the gate, a heavily reinforced structure housed two guards, each carrying AK-47's. This guard house was staffed round the clock every day of the year.

The lodge itself is just over 15 thousand square feet with indoor and outdoor swimming pools, a state of the art fitness facility, and three Jacuzzis. There are a total of 10 bedrooms and 14 bathrooms along with a large and small conference rooms. The grand entry is forty feet wide with a circular staircase leading to the upstairs rooms. A walkway around the perimeter looks down at the opulent great room where massive fireplace stands at the west end of the room with floor to ceiling windows on either side offering breathtaking views of the Montana countryside. Original Remington sculptures and other priceless artwork tastefully adorn walls and shelves throughout the lodge.

Guests are often accompanied by either their girlfriends or hookers flown in from Las Vegas for one of the Senator's lavish weekend parties. Unbeknownst to the guests, each room is equipped with audio and video devices to see, hear and record everything going on in the room. These tapes have been used on more than one occasion to encourage a former houseguest to side with Kingsbury on an issue they may have otherwise been reluctant to support.

The business at hand this weekend was a gathering of oil industry representatives from Iran, Iraq, Kuwait and Saudi Arabia. These countries were the core of the OPEC cartel and each had a special loathing for the United States, some more blatant than others. They also carried the most weight with the other members of OPEC when it came to voting on production quotas. Saudi Arabia, being significantly larger than all the other countries with its oil production, was the biggest hitter in the group. Bryson Chandler was there to represent Global Oil and the Senator's interests. Ballinger was in attendance, but never seen. He spent his time in the tech center of the compound watching all the players enjoying the luxurious accommodations and extracurricular activities provided by the Senator.

The purpose of the gathering was to discuss the continuing support of the OPEC representatives who were providing false data to the analysts at OPEC in Vienna. In exchange for their cooperation Kingsbury had promised to support their representatives in a variety of ways once he was elected President. Despite their mutual dislike for the U.S. all were eager for any help that would help further their own greedy political aspirations. None of them really thought Senator Kingsbury had a chance at becoming the next President of the United States, but they were more than willing to take advantage of his notorious hospitality.

Like so many of their Muslim brethren, the strict laws of the Quran regarding women and alcohol quickly went out the window when they were in the good old US of A. Earlier that afternoon, Kingsbury's private jet had arrived from Las Vegas with four beautiful call girls on board, one for each oil representative. He intentionally snubbed Bryson Chandler who was becoming more and more of an irritant. The little weasel would have to make do on his own. Each lady would earn six thousand dollars for her weekend's activities; an investment the Senator knew would pay huge dividends at a later date. He planned to give each oil representative a gift wrapped video of their nefarious bedroom antics as they departed for their home countries after the weekend meetings. After a lavish dinner that evening each guest retired to his room to find two bottles of 1988 King Brut Vintage champagne chilling by the bedside and a hot Las Vegas hooker warming the sheets. Each man would soon realize just how beholding he was to the Senator and his political aspirations. And each would also correctly assume that a second tape would always be at the Senator's fingertips.

Chapter 22

The long trip back to Houston gave Jack plenty of time to think about all the pieces of the puzzle. Unfortunately, he'd come back with more questions than answers. Who was the guy following him in Vienna? Who did he work for if it wasn't Interpol? What was it that made Trini think the current oil shortage was bogus? Who would most benefit from a bogus oil shortage? Follow the money?

Ballinger sat in his car two blocks away and watched as Jack drove into the apartment complex where Celeste lived. He saw Wilder retrieve a travel bag and a vase of flowers from the back seat of his car. He picked up the phone and called the Senator. "Looks like our friend has been out of town. That explains why I found no sign of him when I went through his girlfriend's apartment. What do you want me to do now?"

"Nothing else for now. Take the next flight out and meet me at the ranch. We have a big meeting to attend with our OPEC guests."

It was just after two in the afternoon. Jack picked up some flowers at the airport and had put them on the coffee table in Celeste's apartment. For some reason he realized that he really missed her while he was in Vienna. He went to the kitchen and got a beer out of the fridge. As he reached for the door he noticed a sticky note on it with a message from Celeste telling him to call Detective Bonham at

Houston PD. Jack downed half the beer and dialed Bonham's number.

"Jack, I was beginning to think you weren't going to call me back," Bonham said as he took a sip of cold coffee and bit into a stale donut.

"You know how it is working for the Government," Jack replied. "They wanted me back at the White House to help the First Lady pick out new china for State Dinners."

"You crack me up. Listen, I may have a lead on your guy with the funny cowboy boots. Name's Cisco Lopeno, some kind of small time drug dealer, but you didn't hear it from me. I'm sure you have the resources to find out where he lives."

"Thanks a lot Bonham, I owe you one," Jack said.

Just as Jack hung up the phone, Celeste came in the door. She gave him a big kiss, took the beer out of his hand and drank what was left of it.

"So, how was your trip? Did you find out anything interesting?" she asked.

"I learned a few things, but first things first." He picked her up like a groom carrying his new bride over the threshold, and practically sprinted into the bedroom where he set her down on the side of the bed. She looked up at him with a wide smile, wrapped her arms around his waist and pulled him down on top of her. They rolled over onto the full length of the bed and quickly went to work on buttons, zippers and general clothing removal.

A half hour later Jack was staring at the ceiling with Celeste resting her head on his chest. He was trying to figure out what he had gotten himself into with this amazing woman. He had mixed feelings about who he was and what he was doing. He wasn't used to caring about someone like he cared about Celeste. After his divorce from his wife, the only one he had any real feelings for was his cat, Angus. He was used to being a loner, with no one to be responsible for except himself, not that he was responsible for Celeste. Quite the opposite actually, she was more than capable of taking care of herself. It was just that he had never felt this way about a woman before.

Celeste got up and went into the kitchen. Jack admired her smooth naked perfect body as she walked away from the bed. She came back with a beer in each hand. She gave one to Jack as she climbed back into bed and slid beneath the sheet. "Jack," she said as she took a sip of her beer, "I need to know where this relationship is going." A sudden fear took over Jack's entire body. He had no idea how to respond. He knew he cared deeply for Celeste but wasn't sure he could ever give her what she wanted. Hell, he didn't even know what that was. He wasn't sure what it was that he wanted. He had no idea where this relationship was headed and wasn't about to go down that road if he could help it. "Well," he said hesitantly," let me ask you this - what do you think would happen if the world ran out of oil?"

"Jack Wilder, what in the hell does that have to do with our relationship?"

"Nothing, but that may have been the reason Trini Palacios was killed."

"You think Palacios discovered the world was running out of oil?" Jack breathed a sigh of relief. It looked like he had successfully dodged the question, at least for now.

"I'm not sure, but that's what one of the guys he worked with at OPEC thought he was working on when he was killed. Not that the world is running out of oil, but that the whole oil shortage thing may be totally made up. The guy worked closely with Palacios and seemed to know what he was talking about."

"I really have no idea what would happen if the world ran out of oil," Celeste said. "Tell me, what else did you learn while you were there? Did you see Inez? How are she and the kids doing?"

Jack spent the next hour filling Celeste in on the details of his trip and getting her opinion on what she thought may be happening. They finished their beers and Celeste again laid her head on Jack's chest. She slowly slid her hand down the inside of his thigh. Things went faster this time, not a lot of clothes to be dealt with.

Chapter 23

Jack sat in his rental car across the street from Cisco's apartment. He was parked under a huge live oak that provided some shade from the oppressive Houston sun. The apartment complex was made up of several buildings, each of which contained four apartments, two up and two down. The landscaping had been neglected and remnants of dead plants and shrubs were everywhere. Kids' bikes in various states of repair were scattered about and a few cars sat on oil slicked driveways. Cisco's place was a lower apartment closest to the street where Jack was parked. He'd been watching for nearly three hours and had seen a variety of people go in and out of Cisco's apartment. These weren't neighbors coming over to borrow a cup of sugar. Bonham was right; the guy was definitely a drug dealer.

A short while later an older model maroon Cadillac arrived. Two giants got out and went into Cisco's place. Both were over six feet, overweight and over ugly. One had a wide nose that seemed to spread clear across his face, must have been broken about a thousand times. The other had a decent nose, but his face sported a scar from just over his right eye all the way down the right side of his face to his chin. He'd obviously found himself on the wrong end of a sharp knife. Both goons had dark skin and black hair that hadn't been close to a barber in several months.

After a few minutes Cisco came out with the two Neanderthals and the three of them drove off in the Caddy. Jack thought Cisco would be a small man based on the size of his ugly boots, and he was right. Cisco was around five-seven give or take, and couldn't have weighed over one-forty soaking wet. He was short and wiry with a neatly trimmed thin mustache. He had a pale, narrow face and small eyes neatly tucked deep into his head.

Jack figured the two giants to be the bookends that held him up while Cisco did his thing that night at the Big Texan. He was a little surprised that such a small guy could pack such a wallop. Maybe the little thug had been a bantam weight boxer before going into the drug business. He watched and waited another half hour then casually let himself into Cisco's apartment. He pulled his Walther out of its holster, took the safety off and jacked a round into the chamber. He'd learned long ago that the two seconds it took to do that put him two seconds ahead of the bad guys when bullets were coming his way.

The first thing Jack saw as he entered the apartment was a huge oil painting hanging on the wall over the fireplace. The painting was an oil on velvet monstrosity of Elvis Presley. He looked around the living room and saw two similar paintings. One was the sad faced clown Emmet Kelly, the other a poor likeness of Willie Nelson. Cisco's bad taste in footwear apparently carried over into the art world as well.

Jack bypassed the kitchen and headed into the master bedroom. The bed was neatly made and covered with a crushed red velvet bedspread. The ceiling above the bed held a huge round mirror.

Across the room was a large, ornately carved oak dresser. The top of the dresser was covered with a variety of bling. Next to one particularly large gold chain was a fully operational lava lamp. *Of course*, Jack thought to himself, *no self-respecting drug dealer would ever be without a lava lamp and a mirror on the ceiling.* He looked in the closet, and there they were, the turquoise boots with the silver tips on the pointed toes, sitting on the floor like two gaudy Andy Warhol paintings. *Bingo*, Jack thought to himself, *a pair of boots like that you just can't forget no matter how hard you try.*

He grabbed a pillow off the bed, removed the red satin pillow case, and carried it and the boots into the kitchen. He cleared everything off the kitchen table and sat the boots in the middle. He opened the refrigerator and found two one quart bottles of Pabst Blue Ribbon beer, yet another example of Cisco's bad taste. Jack poured a full bottle into each boot, threaded the pillow case over them leaving only the silver tips showing and left the apartment.

The next morning he returned to the shade of the live oak and saw pretty much the same activities as the day before. At about the same time as the previous day, the maroon Cadillac returned and the two giants went into Cisco's apartment. A few minutes later the three of them came out; Cisco looked to be in a pretty foul mood, like maybe someone had filled his favorite pair of boots with cheap beer. Once again they all got into the Caddy and left. This time, Jack followed.

They drove just northeast of downtown into Houston's famous Fifth Ward, known for gangs, drugs and other various criminal activities. As they drove down Lavender near Liberty Street, they passed several abandoned buildings, many literally falling apart from neglect. Although the architecture was different, it was eerily similar to some of the war zones Jack had seen in the Middle East. Several houses had broken wooden steps leading up to porches that were either in bad need of repair or already collapsed onto the front yard. There were broken down cars up on blocks in several driveways. Many had missing wheels, others had broken windows, and a few had what looked like bullet holes in the doors. Some of the yards were occupied by small children wearing tattered clothing joyfully playing in dirt yards clogged with weeds and junk.

A few blocks later the trio pulled into the parking lot of a sleazy looking place called the Tijuana Tavern and went inside. Jack could hear loud TexMex music coming from the building as he sat in his car and watched the front door. Several cars drove up over a two hour period with the occupants getting out, going into the bar and returning a short time later. It was clear they weren't there for any of the Tijuana Tavern's exquisite cuisine or exotic cocktails. They were all there for the blue plate special of the day, little packets of white powder they opened and snorted as soon as they got back into their cars.

The parking lot was empty when Jack walked into the dimly lit bar. The joint smelled like fried grease, beer, cigarette smoke and peanuts. He noticed only one customer, who was passed out with his head down on the bar. Aside from Rip Van Winkle, the only other occupants were a tall, skinny, black headed bartender with a big bushy mustache and the two gorillas with Cisco. The bartender was cleaning a row of beer glasses with a rag. He held each one up to the light, carefully studying it as if it were a precious gem before setting it back down on the bar in a neat, orderly fashion. A bartender with a touch of OCD no doubt.

Cisco sat in a booth opposite a pool table behind a stack of cash. The two goons stood flanking him, one on each side. The whole thing looked like something from a Hollywood movie, or maybe from watching one too many Soprano episodes. Jack walked past the pool table and picked the biggest cue stick he could find from the rack on the wall to his right. He racked the balls and centered the cue ball on the table for the break. Just as he thought they would, the two gorillas approached him, one on each side. *This shouldn't be too difficult,* Jack thought to himself, *this time I'm sober and I don't have a hood over my head.*

He waited until they were about five feet away, just a little over the length of a cue stick. He quickly flipped the cue stick around and grabbed it by the narrow end, pivoted on his left foot and hit gorilla number one squarely in the throat. The lug dropped to his knees. Clutched his neck and gasped for breath as Jack adjusted his grip to the middle of the cue stick. He could feel the breath of gorilla number two on the back of his neck. He leaned backward and slammed the end of the stick into the guy's ample mid-section, knocking the wind out of him. Jack turned his attention back to the first guy, smacked him in the side of the head with the cue and he was down for the count. He turned back to gorilla number two whose eyes were bulging as he too gasped for breath and gave him a quick kick to the groin followed by the butt end of the cue stick to the forehead. Two up, two down in less than 10 seconds.

The bartender looked up to see what was going on. Whatever it was, it couldn't be as important as his glass cleaning. He glanced lazily over at Jack, slowly shook his head and went back to drying the row of beer glasses in front of him. A mortified Cisco sprang up like a Jack-in-the-box, stuffed the cash in his pockets and bolted for the door. He made it about halfway when he heard Jack call out "eight ball…corner pocket!" As Cisco started to pick up speed, the eight ball caught him in the back of the head and the lights went out. It was three up, three down in the bottom of the ninth.

Jack sauntered over to Cisco, "game's over, I win," he said as he leaned down grabbed a handful of bills from Cisco's pocket and threw it on the bar. "A tip from Cisco, he wants to thank you for the excellent service," Jack said as he picked Cisco up by one arm and his belt, threw him over his shoulder and walked into the parking lot. He opened the trunk of his rental and tossed Cisco in like a fifty pound bag of chicken feed.

Chapter 24

Azle Iraan, the representative from Saudi Arabia, was the first to enter the conference room after breakfast. He was dressed in a typical Arab Thawb and Keffiyeh. He had deep set eyes, a thick black moustache and goatee covering a strong jaw line. Take away the goatee and he would have been a dead ringer for Omar Sharif in Lawrence of Arabia. His cold steely eyes scanned the room as if looking for some unseen enemy. He did not trust his host and was even less trusting of the other guests attending the meeting. A smartly dressed butler discreetly filled the Wedgewood china cups at each place setting with coffee as the representatives took their seats at the long, ornate table.

"Gentlemen," Kingsbury began, "I trust you all slept well and found the accommodations to your liking." He looked down the long table at the wide smiles as they each nodded in agreement. "Good," he said, "then let's get down to business. I'm sure you all heard about the death of the OPEC analyst in Vienna. What happened to the gentleman was unfortunate but it couldn't be helped. We have a great plan in place and it must not be compromised. That fool was about to ruin everything we've worked for. Fortunately, we found out about it before any real damage was done."

Before anything else was said, Iraan spoke up. "And what of this man, Jack Wilder? What are you doing about him? I understand he has been to Vienna asking lots of questions."

"We are dealing with him" Kingsbury responded. "We had him followed in Vienna. He spotted our man and accosted him in an alley. Wilder bought the story that our guy was from Interpol and had been told to follow him." Kingsbury took a sip of his coffee and looked around the room to gauge any potential discontent before proceeding. "Wilder met with a young OPEC analyst in Vienna named Damon Escobares. Our man in Vienna assured us that Escobares had nothing concrete to offer Wilder. We will continue to monitor Mr. Wilder and deal with him accordingly if the need arises."

"Be that as it may," Iraan responded "he should never have made the trip to Vienna in the first place. There is too much at stake, he should have already been eliminated. Rest assured Senator, if you are unable to handle Wilder we will not hesitate to take matters into our own hands, and believe me, that's the last thing you want us to do."

Arrogant Arab bastard, Kingsbury thought to himself, *you'll change your tune when you see the tape of you and the hooker.*

"I understand Mr. Iraan and as I said, we will continue to monitor the situation with Mr. Wilder and deal with it accordingly."

Just then the crashing of dishes could be heard as Bryson Chandler came staggering into the conference room, spilling half of his Bloody Mary onto the expensive carpet. He had collided with one of the staff carrying a tray of dishes in the hallway.

"Soorrry I'm late boys," Chandler said as he wobbled to his seat, nearly falling twice in the process. Like most drunks, he was having trouble getting one foot in front of the other. "I was bissy trying to talk that cute little souse chef into going for a roll in the hay before the meeting since all the good stuff last night already seemed to be taken." He set his Bloody Mary on the table and promptly knocked it over as he picked up his napkin, oblivious to the spilled drink.

Another member of the staff entered the room and walked directly over to Chandler. "Mr. Chandler, there is an urgent phone call for you. Would you come with me please?" Chandler swayed as he stood and said, "Iss okay boys, carry on, I'll ba ba be back shortly," he slurred as he left the room with a staff member on each side, propping him up as he staggered in the general direction of the door.

"And that's another problem," Iraan said. "How is it that this buffoon is involved and why is he even here?"

"Mr. Chandler is the CEO of Global Oil, who thinks quite highly of himself. He is actually no one of consequence and I assure you he too will be dealt with, and very soon."

With that, Kingsbury proceeded to outline everything he'd put in place to keep the myth of the oil shortage alive. He outlined his relationship with the oil producing countries that weren't represented at his little gathering. He went on to discuss his relationship with the members of the Committee on Energy and Natural Resources and how they were thoroughly convinced that the oil shortage was real.

"As you know, total oil production in the world with full production by all countries is around 84.8 million barrels a day. The world uses around 89 million barrels a day and that's rising, so we're dealing with somewhat of a shortage to begin with." He again looked at his audience to see if there were any comments as he took another sip of his coffee. "So far, Saudi Arabia, Venezuela, Iran and Iraq have cut production by 20 percent. That leaves production down by over 4 million barrels a day. Here in the U.S. Global Oil has totally shut down two wells claiming they have gone dry. This all works very much in our favor.

The country is starting to panic and the Federal Government is on the verge of stepping in. I, of course, will say that's a bad idea and insist the market be allowed to adjust itself. Just after I announce my candidacy for President, I will, at my own expense, visit each one of you in your countries where you will be convinced to open up your vast reserves in the best interest of the world economy." Heads around the room began to nod in agreement. "After that you can slowly increase production back to normal levels under the guise of new discoveries. That will secure my candidacy for President, both as a world leader and a diplomat."

Chapter 25

The bucket of ice water thrown in his face brought Cisco back to the land of the living. As he looked up, he realized he was sitting upright in a wooden chair with his hands and feet tightly bound to the chair with duct tape. Another strip of duct tape covered his mouth. As he opened his eyes all he could see was a bright light shining directly at him. He had no idea where he was. The blinding light heightened the intensity of his throbbing headache.

The last thing he remembered was collecting his money and trying to make a quick exit from his "office" at the Tijuana tavern. He closed his eyes to block out the light and the pain in his head. He held his breath and cocked his head sideways to get a better sense of where he was. He listened for a moment and could hear someone breathing close by.

"So, my little friend, we meet again," Wilder said as he slowly walked in a semi-circle behind Cisco. "Only this time I don't have a bag over my head and you don't have your two gorilla sidekicks to do your dirty work for you. It looks like it's just you and me." Jack reached over and ripped the tape off Cisco's mouth.

"You got the wrong guy, pendejo," Cisco said. "I got no idea what you're talking about."

"Wrong thing to say moron!" Jack yelled as he slapped the back of Cisco's head. Cisco yelped in pain. It felt like a nail had been driven into his already tender head. "Let me just ask you this, Cisco. Where do you want me to send the pieces?"

"Pieces, what pieces? What the hell are you talking about man?"

"I'm talking about your body. I'm going to chop you into little pieces. You're going to look like an unsolvable jigsaw puzzle when I'm done. I'm thinking your scrawny little body will probably fit into a pretty small box when I'm finished. So, where do you want me to send the body puzzle pieces? Or, should I just take them out in the desert and scatter them for the buzzards. It's up to you."

Jack moved around to the front of the chair. He paused a moment to be sure Cisco got a good look at the shiny new meat cleaver he was holding. Cisco began to sweat and his lips began to quiver. Jack slammed the cleaver down into the arm of the wooden chair. The blade stuck a fraction of an inch from Cisco's right hand. Cisco's face went pale and his heart started pounding as if it would explode. "Okay, okay!" Cisco said, "I'll tell you whatever you want to know, just get that thing away from me."

It was an interrogation method Jack had used many times - bright lights, disorientation, cold water and a meat cleaver. It always worked. Once in awhile it cost the detainee a finger or two, but it always worked in the end.

"Okay, smart guy," Jack said, "let's start by you telling me who sent you and your goons to run me out of town."

"Chandler, Bryson Chandler, works at Global Oil, downtown Houston in the Williams Tower," Cisco babbled. "He hired me and the guys to follow you, rough you up and tell you to get outta Dodge. He paid us five grand and promised another five when you left town. If you want, me and the guys can go beat him up for you. It will only cost you five grand, okay, maybe four grand if that's better for you or maybe free…We can do it for free if you want, just let me go."

Suddenly Cisco was a fountain of information and wouldn't shut up. "Cisco," Jack shouted, "just shut up and calm down." Cisco stopped and took a deep breath, wondering if it was going to be his last. "Now, what can you tell me about Trinidad Palacios and Garrison Shepherd?"

"I don't know nobody named Palacios…I mean I know lots of guys named Palacios, just not that *particular* Palacios dude. You know what I'm sayin? The Shepherd guy I read about in the newspaper. Word on the street is that he got whacked by some guy from Chicago but I don't know for sure. I swear man, that's all I know, just that and the stuff about the Chandler guy. Now can I go?"

Jack slowly walked behind Cisco, unplugged the light and sat down on the floor. The room was completely dark. The only noise was the sound of

Cisco's moaning. "Hey man, what you gonna do now?" Cisco asked.

"Quiet, I'm thinking," Jack replied. After several minutes he stood and plugged the light back in. "Cisco, my fine little hoodlum friend, this is your lucky day. I don't want you to beat anybody up, I want you to do a little research for me."

"What? You mean like book research and stuff like that? I don't know nothing about no book research."

"No Cisco, this kind of research is more in line with what you usually do in your particular kind of nefarious endeavors."

"I don't know nothing about no numerous endovers man, I just help get people beat up and sell some drugs now and then. I'm more in the line of what you call persuasion, know what I mean?"

"No Cisco, *I'm in the line of persuasion*. You're just a little drug dealing weasel with really, really bad taste in clothes, furniture, artwork and beer. Now, listen carefully, I'm only going to say this once. I want you to find out about this guy from Chicago. I want to know who he is and who hired him to kill Shepherd. Exactly one week from today I will meet you at that dive tavern where I found you. I will have people watching you. If you try to leave town I will have you killed. If you try to have anything done to me I will have you killed. If you aren't there next week, I will hunt you down and kill you myself. I will start by cutting off your fingers with this handy dandy meat cleaver and working my way up to your neck. Comprende amigo?"

Jack took the razor sharp cleaver and cut the tape to free Cisco's right arm, then, he unplugged the light again, leaving Cisco in the dark. He walked across the room and turned on the overhead light in the living room of Cisco's apartment. "See you next week," he said as he closed the door behind him.

Chapter 26

There was a slight chill in the air and a strong breeze bent the tree tops as Jack sat in his car mulling over the information he'd just pried out of Cisco. He rolled his window down and drew in a deep breath of the cool air. He hoped it would help clear his mind as he wondered why Chandler wanted him to stay away from investigating the death of Garrison Shepherd. Surely Global Oil was not behind Garrison's death, or were they? Jack was still in a quandary about what kind of a connection there could be between the deaths of Garrison Shepherd and Trini Palacios. Could Global have been involved in both murders? What was it Cisco had said about Garrison's death? "Word on the street is that he got whacked by some guy from Chicago." What kind of stuff would Garrison have been involved in at Global that would have gotten him killed?

Jack had a good friend from college, Gordon Mansfield. Gordo and Jack had taken several classes together. The difference being that Gordo was there to learn while Jack was there to party. They had remained good friends for a few years after Jack was asked to leave that particular university, then marriage and life had intervened and they drifted apart. Gordo had graduated with a degree in criminology and Jack heard that he had become a detective in the Chicago PD. Time to renew an old acquaintance.

Jack dialed the non-emergency number of the Chicago Bureau of Detectives. A gruff sounding

140

Sergeant answered, "Detective Bureau, Sergeant Crosby speaking."

"Sergeant, my name is Jack Wilder. I'm looking for a detective Gordon Mansfield, I don't know which district he may be attached to."

"That would be Gordo Mansfield sir. He works out of the Calumet Division over in the Fifth District. Gordo and I actually started in the Chicago PD on the same day. I know him well. He isn't available though, he works a night shift. Is there anything I can help you with?"

"I see his nickname stuck with him all these years," Jack said. "He and I are old college buddies. I was just trying to get in touch to talk about old times and catch up."

Jack gave the sergeant his number and asked him to have Gordo give him a call.

The cold wind had turned into a light rain and then a downpour by the time Jack pulled into the parking lot at Celeste's apartment. He made a mad dash for the front door, dropped his wet coat in the hall and headed for the fridge. He had just opened his first beer when his cell phone rang.

"Jackson Wilder, you old son-of-a-gun, how the heck are you? What in the world have you been doing for the last 10 years?" It was Gordo returning his call.

"Well I could tell you Gordo, but then I would have to kill you. A lot of it has been secret government stuff."

"Seriously?"

"Well, not totally," Jack replied. "I spent a little time in the military, then some time with the CIA, left the CIA and now I call myself a consultant to the U.S. Government. I hire myself out to a lot of different government agencies, at least that's the story I'm supposed to tell."

"Sounds fun."

"It has its ups and downs. What about you? Sounds as though you have done pretty well for yourself Mr. Big shot detective." Jack leaned against the fridge and took a drink of the cold beer.

"Yeah, I guess so" Gordo replied. "The PD has been good to me. I get to chase bad guys, get shot at once in awhile, solve a murder now and then. Never a dull moment until I have to sit down at the end of a bust and fill out about ninety thousand reports."

"Sounds a lot like what I do, but without the tedious report writing. Nobody in my world wants anything on paper."

"So, what can I do for you my friend?"

Jack took another swallow of beer, walked into the living room, sat down on the couch, kicked off his shoes and put his feet up on the coffee table. "Do you remember Garrison Shepherd from college?" He asked.

"Sure I do, he went drinking with us a few times. You and he were pretty close as I recall."

"We were indeed. I was best man at his wedding not long ago."

"So what's he up to these days? I heard he had something to do with the oil business and had moved to Texas."

"That's true," Jack said. "He worked for a company in Houston called Global Oil. He was murdered a few weeks ago. It happened shortly after a guy he had worked with at Global was assassinated at a press conference in Vienna. This guy, Trinidad Palacios, had worked with Garrison at Global before going to work for OPEC in Vienna."

"Whoa, Jack, that's terrible. I am so sorry about Garrison. What can I do to help you? Just name it."

Jack filled Gordo in on everything he had managed to find out about both murders, which wasn't much, and about Garrison marrying Angelina whom no one liked and the fact that she had apparently moved from Chicago to Houston after her wealthy real estate magnate husband died of a heart attack. "I had a recent conversation with a two bit drug dealer here in Houston who said the word on the street was that Garrison was a contract hit by someone from Chicago."

"Most of the hit men I'm familiar with here in Chicago are somehow associated with the big Italian crime families. But I'm sure there are a few freelancers out there. I also seem to recall something awhile back about some big shot real estate tycoon having a heart attack at a private club downtown. Let me do some digging and I will get back to you."

The next call Jack made was to Donna Crowley at Global Oil. "Donna, Jack Wilder calling. Listen, can you think of a reason Chandler would have hired some guys to beat me up and try to get me to leave town?"

"My goodness, no Jack! Are you okay?"

"I'm fine thanks. I'm going to drop in tomorrow and pay Mr. Chandler a little visit."

"Don't bother Jack, he isn't here. He got called out of town. Said he was going to visit some Senator at a ranch in Montana."

"Do you know who this Senator is? Jack asked.

"Hold on and I'll check his personal calendar on his desk." Donna put Jack on hold and hurried into her boss's office. She knew he kept his personal calendar in the locked right hand drawer of his opulent desk. She also knew he kept the key under the plant on the shelf of his credenza.

"Got it," she said as she picked up the phone. "His calendar says he's at Senator Kingsbury's ranch until Tuesday of next week."

"Thanks a lot Donna, I'll see you Wednesday of next week," Jack said as hung up.

Chapter 27

Bryson Chandler poured himself another glass of cheap Scotch out of the bottle in his room. His room was the smallest in the compound, located at the far end of the hallway leading to the guestrooms. He'd been locked in since being escorted out of the meeting that morning under the pretext of taking an urgent call. He sat on the bed sulking and sipping. *Here I am, while those arrogant Arab bastards had better rooms, better liquor and of course female companionship for their horizontal refreshment and entertainment. I deserve better than this,* Chandler thought to himself as he poured his fourth glass. *I made a fortune for that bastard Kingsbury and this is all he thinks of me! I took Global from a small nothing of an oil company and turned it into a conglomerate worth billions!*

He got up off the bed, walked across the room and tried the door. Still locked. He banged on the door and shouted "I know what Senator Hamilton Kingsbury the friggin third is up to and I'm gonna tell the whole damn world."

Kingsbury and Ballinger watched Chandler on the large monitor in the tech center. "I believe Mr. Chandler has become more of a liability than an asset," Kingsbury said as he looked up from the monitor. "Please deal with him accordingly and add it to your fee." Ballinger smiled and nodded as Kingsbury left the room. While Ballinger certainly wasn't fond of the Senator, he liked Bryson Chandler even less. He thought of Chandler as an overbearing, stuck up, pretentious ass. *Actually, except for a few billion dollars, there isn't that much difference between those two.*

Ballinger left the main house and walked across the compound to the maintenance area where the ranch hands kept their tools. He looked around to see if anyone had noticed him and ducked into the side door of the maintenance garage. He rummaged through a toolbox and found a small set of wire cutters that were perfect for what he had in mind. He tucked the wire cutters in his jacket pocket and walked across the compound to where the vehicles were kept.

Once again he looked around to see if he had been noticed, then quickly stepped inside. He looked down the row of cars and spotted Chandler's rented S550 Mercedes sedan. At a cost of close to a hundred thousand bucks he wondered what the daily rental was on a car like this. *I wonder if he bought the extra insurance,* Ballinger thought as he crawled beneath the car and cut the brake lines about a fourth of the way through.

Ballinger figured the car could go about three miles before it was completely without brakes, less if he pumped the brakes much going into the curves. He grabbed the keys to the Mercedes off the key rack, got in it, and slowly drove to the front door of the main house where he coasted to a stop without touching the brakes. He got out of the expensive set of wheels, opened the main door and walked down the long hallway to the last room on the right where

Chandler had been taken. He could hear incoherent banging and swearing as he approached the door to the drunken CEO's room.

Ballinger unlocked the door with his master key and gave it a quick shove. The door caught Chandler square in the face. He stumbled backwards several steps and landed on the bed. Ballinger put his nose about three inches from Chandler's and gave him a cold hard stare. The guy smelled like the inside of a cheap bottle of Scotch and his bloodshot eyes looked like a Rand McNally road map. His left eye had begun to swell from the encounter with the door. Ballinger knew Chandler would be intimidated, drunk or not.

"Senator Kingsbury feels that your presence is no longer required at this meeting" he said without taking his eyes off Chandler's. "Your car is out front and the Senator's private jet is waiting for you at the airport. The pilot will take you directly to Houston." He handed Chandler the keys and yanked him up off the bed. Ballinger looked down the hall to make sure no one was watching. He held Chandler firmly by the arm to steady him as they made their way down the hall and out the front door. Chandler was strangely silent as they made their way down the long hall.

Ballinger pulled his sunglasses from his pocket, squinted and put them on as they stepped out into the bright sunshine. It was the middle of March and there were still patches of snow on the ground. The reflection was hard on the eyes, something Chandler didn't seem to notice. Ballinger opened the door to the Mercedes and helped Chandler get in. He didn't bother with the seatbelt and neither did Chandler. "Have a nice trip," Ballinger said as he closed the door to the big sedan.

Chandler started the car and promptly backed into a trash can. In his mind, Ballinger rehearsed what he would later say to the authorities. "I told him he was in no shape to drive, but he insisted on leaving and wouldn't give me his keys. He got into the car and locked the door before I had a chance to do anything."

Ballinger walked to the phone in the lobby and dialed the Senator's room. "Mr. Chandler should no longer be a problem" he said.

"Good" Kingsbury replied. "Now, head back to Houston and see what's going on there."

Somehow Chandler managed to get the gear shift from reverse into drive and slowly drove off. Ballinger picked up the nearest house phone, called the front gate and told the guard that Chandler was on his way. He gave instructions for the guard to wave him through without stopping him.

As Chandler passed the guard house he stomped down on the accelerator and the big Mercedes took off like a rocket. The car handled like a race car on the first curve despite Chandler's condition. As he entered the third curve and the steepest downgrade the sun and snow were starting to affect his vision. He tapped the brakes to slow down. Nothing happened.

He pushed the brake pedal all the way to the floor, still nothing.

Chandler's mind was having a difficult time processing what was happening. He couldn't quite figure out where he was, it felt like some kind of strange dream. He turned the wheel sharply to the right and the huge sedan plowed through the guard rail. The airbag inflated and deflated while Chandler was airborne. As he looked out the side window and saw the clouds on the horizon he thought he was in the private jet headed for Houston.

The Mercedes hit an outcropping of rocks about a hundred feet down the canyon and flipped end over end several times before hitting the ground again and rolling the rest of the way to the bottom of the canyon. Somewhere about halfway to the bottom, Chandler had been ejected. They found his body nearly three hundred feet from the mangled Mercedes two days later.

Chapter 28

Jack and Celeste were enjoying a leisurely, late Sunday morning breakfast. Jack had gotten up early, made coffee, poured orange juice and was now working on the eggs. He handed Celeste a cup of coffee as she sat down at the kitchen table. "Wow, and he can cook too! Play your cards right mister and this could turn into something big," she said as Jack's cell phone rang. She got up to tend the eggs while Jack took his cup of coffee and sat down at the table to take the call.

He listened as Gordo filled him in on what he'd found out about the late Bardwell Bishop of Chicago. Bishop had indeed been a very wealthy real estate developer and died suddenly of a heart attack while having drinks with friends at a very exclusive private club. Sometime before that he had married a much younger woman. A woman that none of his friends or business associates seemed to care for. There were even a few rumors that the new young wife was having an affair with her tennis instructor, or trainer, or pool boy, or someone like that, but nothing conclusive.

A routine investigation was done regarding Bishop's death. Other members of the exclusive club were interviewed at length in their various mansions and opulent offices. They were all aware that Bishop had a bad ticker and a tendency to drink, eat and smoke too much. He seemed like an old guy trying to live a collegiate lifestyle, one that included late night partying and the pursuit of young, voluptuous women. The fact that he was married didn't seem to hamper his lust for the opposite sex. The old guy no doubt had a few affairs of his own. Some of his friends were aware he had been taking some kind of heart medication. All in all, no one was surprised when the guy had kicked the bucket. Everyone had spoken highly of him.

There was mention of a client Bishop introduced to his friends that night, but no one could remember much about him, not even his name. A couple of people said he just kind of vanished when Bardwell hit the floor and no one paid any more attention to him in the ensuing chaos of calling 911, doing CPR, the paramedics arriving and so on.

The guy who interviewed the widow Bishop said she didn't seem too upset. A few months later she sold the Chicago mansion and left town. Seems that most of her husband's money was tied up in several different trusts and most of it went to various charities. Maybe he wasn't as dumb as some of his friends thought. No one knew or cared where she went.

"I dug a little deeper and found that Mr. Bishop had taken out a substantial life insurance policy to the tune of two million shortly after they were married," Gordo said. "Add to that the fact that the old geezer, married or not, liked to chase women and it isn't a far stretch to make a case for a jealous wife with a motive for murder. It certainly wouldn't be the first time jealousy and money led to murder."

Celeste put a plate of eggs in front of Jack and he took a couple bites as he continued to listen to Gordo. "I haven't had much luck running down any freelance guys who work outside of organized crime," Gordo continued, "But I did come across one person of interest. A guy named Carmine Milano. He was implicated in a murder for hire plot a couple years back, but they were never able to pin it on him. The fly in the ointment with this whole thing Jack, is the coroner's report on Bishop, it clearly says heart attack."

Jack nodded his head, said "Hmm," and took a sip of coffee and another bite of his eggs.

"So let me ask you this Gordo, is there a way to check up on where this Carmine Milano guy may have been around the time Garrison was killed?"

"I'm a step ahead of you on that one my friend. I had one of the detectives over in the eighth district ask around. He found out from one of his confidential informants that one Carmine Milano took a flight out of O'Hare to Houston the night before Garrison was killed. Pretty circumstantial given the coroner's report, but still a pretty valuable piece of information."

"Gordo, you are a prince. I owe you big time. Someday when they make a movie about my life, I will insist that you play me. Just think of it, Hollywood, hot tubs, lots of booze and hot and cold running women."

"Thanks Jack, but I prefer my dull boring life of chasing bad guys and getting shot at once in awhile just to keep my heart rate up. Besides, I would really miss the winter blizzards of Chicago."

Jack thanked Gordo again, they swapped a few more stories about the old college days and promised to keep in touch.

Chapter 29

The sun was setting and a warm breeze was wafting in from the south as Jack walked into the bar. The western sky was awash with red and yellow clouds. *You just can't beat a Texas sunset,* Jack thought to himself as he walked through the doors. Cisco was sat in his usual place with his two gorillas standing in front of him. They looked like a pair of Pillsbury dough boys in cowboy boots. As Jack approached Cisco the dough boys moved away giving him a wide berth. They both sported huge bruises on their faces that were in that stage where they start to change from purple to a bluish yellow, trophies from their recent encounter with Jack.

Cisco waved at the bartender who brought two bottles of Pabst Blue Ribbon beer over and set them on the table. Jack picked one up, looked at Cisco and just shook his head. He handed the bottle back to the bartender and asked for a Shiner Bock. Then he sat back in his chair, looked Cisco directly in the eyes and said "So, what have you got for me my fine little felonious friend?" Cisco took a sip of Pabst, leaned forward and looked around as if he wanted to make sure no one was listening. Aside from the gorillas and the bartender, he and Jack were the only ones in the joint.

"I talked to some guys who know some guys. I mean I move a few drugs now and then, but these dudes are some heavy hitters, you know what I mean? The word is, this guy Garrison's killing was definitely a contract hit made by some dude out of Chicago. Everyone thinks his wife ordered the hit."

"His wife," Jack said. "Are you sure? How reliable are your sources?"

"Pretty reliable, and let me tell you something bro, these are the kind of guys you don't want to go messing around with."

Jack took a sip of Shiner and stared at Cisco, watching his eyes to see if the little drug dealing rat was telling the truth. Jack thought he probably was telling the truth. The more he thought about it, the more it seemed to make sense, especially with the information he had received from Gordo. At first he had been pretty sure there must be a connection to Trini's death. And, maybe there was, although he couldn't really see some hit man from Chicago travelling to Vienna to kill Trini. For that to have happened, there would have been a connection between what Garrison was working on and what Trini had been working on, and there didn't seem to be one. *Could it be that Angelina had been responsible for the death of two husbands?*

"Cisco, my man," Jack said, "You've done well. Now I'm going to give you some advice. Get out of the drug business and move somewhere far away. If these guys are as bad as you say they are, they will come looking for you and they won't be looking for information. They will be looking to kill you. They don't like loose ends."

"That ain't gonna happen bro, I got a good gig going here and my boys here can take good care of me," Cisco said as he crossed his arms and pointed at the two gorillas. "As long as you don't rat me out to the cops, I'll be fine."

"They didn't do a very good job of taking care of you the last time I was here," Jack said as he stood and headed for the door. "I'm as serious as a heart attack Cisco, get out while you can. You will never see these guys coming." Jack didn't bother to look back. His business with Cisco was done.

"Guy don't know what he's talking about," Cisco said to no one in particular. "As long as business is good, I'm good, and I ain't leavin." An hour or so after Jack left, Cisco was open for business. Several of his regular customers began to drift in for their weekly fix. Business was good and the cash register was singing. Cisco smiled with each transaction and with each transaction he stuffed a wad of cash into his pocket. The gorillas on either side of him carefully looked over everyone who came in the bar that night.

It was a little after two in the morning when Cisco and his two goons left the bar. As they walked outside, Cisco looked up at the clear Texas sky, took a deep breath of fresh air and said, "It's a great night to be alive and rich ain't it boys?" The three of them walked across the dusty, deserted parking lot and had just reached their car when Cisco heard the first two pops. The giant bodyguard standing to Cisco's left grimaced in pain and his eyes opened wide as he slowly looked down at his chest. A crimson stain was growing, pumping its way from beneath the fabric onto the man's chest just below the pocket line of his gaudy blue and white cowboy shirt. The blood ran down his shirt dripping onto the toes of his equally gaudy cowboy boots. The man's knees buckled and he fell forward hitting the dirt like a giant Douglas fir falling in the forest. Gorilla number two quickly reached inside his jacket for his gun and spun in two complete circles, gun in hand, searching for the source of the shots. As he frantically looked around, two more pops came from nowhere. Another crimson stain, another tree falls in the forest. Cisco stood frozen with fear, he remembered Jack's warning, "They don't like loose ends."

The shooter appeared like a ghostly apparition, materializing out of nowhere, slowly walking from the darkness into the light from the far side of the parking lot. He casually approached Cisco, his gaze never leaving the drug dealer's eyes. Cisco's mind said run, but his body remained frozen, his heart racing in his chest like the churning wheels of a runaway locomotive. He had no weapon of his own, always confident that his two boys could handle anything that came their way. He just stood there, like a short ice statue wearing ugly cowboy boots.

The stranger was about five-ten with a full head of medium length black hair combed straight back. He had a narrow, slightly bent nose that held court over thin, nearly invisible lips. His eyes were tiny black coals that seemed to have a touch of red in the center of the pupils. He was wearing a black, high neck sweater under a black full length leather coat, black pants and black shoes with pointed tips. He blended perfectly with the cold dark night, looking like the devil himself. His eyes never moved or blinked. They seemed to look straight through Cisco.

"Hello Cisco" the shooter said. "My name is Carmine. I heard you were asking about me. You shouldn't have done that my friend. You're way out of your league." Those were the last words Cisco Lopeno ever heard. There was one more pop disturbing the stillness of the night. The little hoodlum never felt the nine millimeter bullet push into his head, dead center, just above the bridge of his nose. Everything turned black as the bullet's momentum pushed him back against the side of the car. Blood oozed from his forehead, down his nose, and dripped onto his shirt like a leaky faucet, drip, drip. His body slowly edged down the side of the car door to the ground as his legs buckled under the dead weight of his scrawny frame. He came to a stop in a sitting position between his two dead bodyguards.

His work done, Carmine looked around, picked the ejected brass casing out of the dirt, turned and casually walked across the desolate parking lot, fading back into the dark night. He had one more Texas target on his list to deal with before heading home to Chicago.

Chapter 30

Celeste was sitting on the couch reading a magazine when Jack walked in. "Let me see your gun," she said as she looked up at him.

"What?

"I said, let me see your gun."

"Celeste, it's not a toy. It's a tool, a tool of my trade unfortunately."

"Don't make me ask again cowboy, just let me see the damn gun."

Jack reached under his jacket and pulled the Walther PPK from his shoulder holster. He walked over and pulled the clip from the weapon as he eased down beside her on the couch. He pulled the slide back ejecting the round from the chamber and handed her the gun.

"Hmmm," she said as she slid her hand up one side of the barrel and down the other to the grip, caressing the weapon. She slowly turned it over in her soft hands a couple of times, her eyes scanning every inch of it. "Teach me to shoot it," she said, "or one like it."

"What on earth for?" Jack asked.

"Because I'm afraid of it and I don't want to be," she said. "I grew up with a dad and two brothers with guns, but they were mostly rifles and shotguns they used for hunting. They told me guns weren't for girls and said I should be afraid of them, so I guess I always was." She turned the gun over once more in her hands and handed it back to Jack. "If we are going to have a relationship that means I have to be around you and your gun and I don't want to be afraid of either one. I want you to teach me how to shoot one, and I want to own one, maybe a Walter PBJ, just like this one."

"It's not Walter, it's Walther, and it's not a PBJ, it's a PPK," Jack said as he pushed the clip back into the grip, pumped a round into the chamber, and clicked the safety on.

"What's that thing you just did, sliding that piece back?"

"Sliding the top of the barrel back pushes a bullet into the chamber of the gun, so it's ready to fire if you need it."

"Wouldn't it be safer to carry around if there wasn't a bullet in it?" she asked.

"Here's the thing," Jack replied. "It takes a fraction of a second to jack a round into the chamber. If the bad guy is pointing a gun at you and he already has one in the chamber, his bullet is going to be a fraction of a second faster than yours, assuming you get the chance to fire your weapon at him. Unless he's a pretty bad shot, he's going to be pretty busy killing you while you are trying to chamber a round."

"I guess that makes sense," she said as she watched Jack pull his coat open and put the Walther back into his shoulder holster. "It's a lot heavier than I thought it would be."

"There are all kinds of guns out there to choose from, some heavier, some lighter, some bigger, some smaller. The Walther PPK is one of several that I own."

Celeste pushed off the couch and went into the kitchen. She came back with a chilled bottle of Chardonnay and two glasses. She poured them each a glass, tucked her feet up under her on the couch and leaned on Jack resting her head on his shoulder. "I really do want to learn how to shoot," she said, "and I think you are the only one I would trust to teach me."

"Okay, I'll tell you what," Jack said as he took a sip of wine. "Why don't we sleep on it and if you feel the same way tomorrow we'll go find a shooting range and see what you think after you've pulled the trigger a few times."

"Deal!" she said as she snuggled a little closer and kissed Jack on the cheek.

They finished the bottle and Celeste went to bed. Jack stayed up late mulling over the events of the day and what he'd learned from Cisco. It certainly made some degree of sense that Angelina could or would have hired someone to kill Garrison. He knew he'd put off the inevitable long enough. After tomorrow's trip to the shooting range he would pay the grieving widow a visit. For a moment, he even thought about leaving his gun with Celeste to lessen his temptation to do the world a favor by killing the woman.

Jack opened another bottle of Chardonnay, grabbed a pen and paper from his briefcase and sat down at the kitchen table to make a few notes. He wrote the word FACTS at the top of a blank page, underlined it and started a list. 1. OPEC analyst assassinated in Vienna, why? Assailant unknown 2. Someone followed me in Vienna, hired by who? 3. Damon Escobares thought Trini was suspicious of the oil shortage, why? 4. Trini wanted his wife to send a package to Garrison. 5. Garrison killed in Houston, hired gun from Chicago, or did it have something to do with what Trini sent him? 6. Did Cisco really know what he was talking about? 7. Bryson Chandler hired Cisco to get me to leave town, why?

Jack stared at the list, trying to connect the dots. The wine was making the dots start to blur. He decided to call it a night and start again the next day with a clearer head. He crawled beneath the covers next to a softly snoring Celeste. *Hmmm snoring, I never knew she snored. Probably dreaming of shooting it out with the some bad guys,* he thought to himself as he settled in and drifted off.

Chapter 31

The next morning Jack woke to the smell of coffee brewing and breakfast cooking. Celeste rose early in her eagerness to go to the shooting range.

"So, are we still going to do it?' Celeste asked a groggy Jack as he shuffled into the kitchen.

"Do what?" Jack said as he poured a cup of coffee.

"Well, go to the shooting range of course!"

"So after sleeping on it, you still want to go?"

"More than ever."

"Okay then, that's what we'll do."

Carmine was parked about halfway down the block. He'd come to Houston to tie up loose ends. He watched Jack and Celeste in his mirror as they got into her Lexus and drove past him. Carmine had gotten a call from one of his people in Houston telling him that some small time drug dealer named Cisco Lopeno had been asking around about the death of Angelina's Bishop-Shepherd's second husband. The guy also told Carmine that a guy named Jack Wilder was the one pushing Lopeno for information.

Carmine had turned down Angelina Bishop's request to kill her second husband and the guy ended

up dead anyway. He killed her first husband and got away clean, but there was something about Angelina that bothered him. She just seemed a little....weird somehow. With her second husband dead, he knew a lot of questions could lead back to him, especially if those questions led the cops to Angelina
.

Killing Cisco and his pals had been an easy task. The guy was dumb, small time, careless, and lazy. Carmine's focus was now on Wilder. He'd been in the business long enough to know this wouldn't be an ordinary hit. He could tell by the way Wilder carried himself that the guy was a player. He was sharp, alert, smart, a cop maybe. He always went with his instincts and he knew he needed to find out a little more about his prey before plotting a course of action.

The Top Gun shooting range on Beverly Hill road in Houston, not far from Memorial Park, is one of the highest rated ranges in the area. It looks like an old warehouse converted into a shooting range with 15 shooting lanes and nearly that many bad guy targets that can be attached to trolleys and carried up to fifty feet away. Nearly every weapon imaginable from .22 caliber handguns to fully automatic class III Uzis are available to rent.

Jack chose three weapons with 10 rounds of ammo for each one. He picked out the most menacing of the bad guy targets for Celeste to shoot at. He chose a Sig Sauer 522, 22 caliber handgun as a starting point for her. He positioned Celeste in front of him with his arms around her. He showed her how to properly hold the weapon with her trigger finger straight out, resting on the trigger guard. He explained the proper way to grip the weapon in the web of her right hand, while cupping her left hand around her right, cradling the weapon for stability. He stepped back and let her drop her hand to her side then raise and cradle the weapon several times to get a feel for it. Next he showed her the proper stance, feet shoulder width apart, left foot slightly ahead of the right. He explained that the right arm should be straight with the left elbow slightly bent for maximum control.

After having her practice raising the weapon, aiming it and going into the proper stance a few times, he loaded the Sig and ran the target out. They put on their mandatory noise protection headsets, and he told her to "fire away." She looked blankly at him for just an instant, swallowed hard and moved carefully into the new stance and position she'd just rehearsed. The first shot went high and into the wall behind the target. The next shot went left and into the wall. Jack stepped behind her and repositioned the weapon properly in her hands. He placed his long arms around hers and helped her steady the weapon. He loved the feel of her body against his, the smell of her hair, the nape of her neck. His mind began to wander to other parts of her body. He took a deep breath to get back on track and told her to focus on where the front site of the gun was pointed. He lifted the ear piece away from her left ear. "Concentrate on your breathing," he whispered into her ear. "The key is to pull the trigger when you exhale."

He stepped back and watched her place the next two rounds into the perimeter of the target. Better. She took two deep breaths, then fired three quick shots. Though none were kill shots, they all three hit the target. While the bad guy would no doubt live to fight another day, he probably had a flesh wound or two.

Next, Jack picked up the .357 Glock 32 and handed it to her. This gun proved to be too much for her. The recoil pushed her way off balance. Moving from a gun with very little recoil to one with lots of recoil was too much of a jump. He reached under his jacket, pulled his Walther out of the holster and handed it to her. She gave Jack a serious look. "Really?" she said. "So soon?" Jack gave her a half smile and nodded toward the target. She quickly realized it wasn't as comfortable as the Sig 22, but still a better fit than the Glock .357. Six more shots; four misses, two hits.

They finished with a 9 millimeter Glock 26. Often called the Baby Glock, this was the smallest and most compact of the four weapons. After shooting the Glock 26 and hitting the target with 6 of the 10 rounds, Celeste turned to Jack. "Just like Goldilocks said, this one is just right," she beamed.

"I thought you might like it," Jack replied as they gathered the weapons and headed back to the front desk. "You have to remember though, six out of 10 isn't good enough in a real firefight, especially if the bad guy can hit 10 out of 10."

When they returned to Celeste's apartment Jack sat down on the couch and pulled his right pants leg up. He unstrapped his hidden ankle holster and handed it to Celeste with the Glock 26 strapped in. "Here you go," he said. "Try and get to the practice range as often as you can. You probably should shoot a few hundred more rounds. You need to be able to do 10 out of 10 every time without even thinking about it."

"You've had this thing with you all the time you've been here?"

"There are just some things a guy just doesn't tell a girl," Jack said with a smile.

Celeste took the Glock 26 into her bedroom and placed it gently on her dresser. She took a minute to stare at the weapon. She was thinking about picking it up again when she heard the door bell ring.

The first thing she saw when she opened the door was a detective badge in a holder being held up to her face. The guy behind the badge was several inches short of the six foot mark and looked to be about as wide as he was tall. Apparently the Houston Police Department didn't have an annual physical agility test detectives had to pass. If there were, this guy must have found a way to cheat his way around it. He was wearing a wrinkled gray shirt, a food-stained red tie, wrinkled gray slacks and a navy sports jacket that seemed to be at least one size too small. His face was pale, baby smooth and almost perfectly round, kind of a Charlie Brown face.

"Ms. Windom? Detective Glen Rose. I'm with the Houston Police Department. May I come in?" he asked as he walked past her without waiting for an answer. Celeste quickly stepped aside to avoid being crushed by the portly detective as he brushed past her. "I'm looking for a Jack Wilder."

"That would be me detective, what can I do for you?" Jack called from the couch as he shifted his weight to get more comfortable.

"What can you tell me about your relationship with Cisco Lopeno?"

"I am acquainted with Mr. Lopeno, but I don't know what you mean by relationship," Jack said as he took off his shoes and put his feet up on the coffee table.

"When was the last time you saw him?"

"I would have to give that some thought and have a look at my calendar," Jack replied. "I keep a pretty hectic schedule going to museums, political fundraisers, skydiving, racing cars, designing furniture, going to book clubs, and so on.

"Very funny Wilder," Rose responded as he plopped his huge frame down onto an adjacent chair.

"What I heard was that the two of you *weren't* very good friends. In fact, what I heard was that the two of you actually didn't really like each other at all."

"Not true," Jack replied, "I'm really a very likeable guy, ask anybody."

"What about Lopeno's two body guards? How well did you get along with them?"

"Oh, is that what those guys were? I thought they were cousins or brothers or something. They never spoke much as I recall."

"So tell me Jack, where were you around midnight last night?" Rose asked as he shifted his huge frame in the shrinking chair.

"In that room right there," Jack pointed across the living room to the bedroom. "Sound asleep. It's what I to do most nights around midnight."

With a huge effort Rose hoisted himself out of the chair, took a deep breath and meandered around the room looking at pictures on the wall. "I understand you work for the government," he said." What is it that do for our fine country?" Rose stopped and stared at a large elegantly framed photo of Celeste and her family.

"Oh, you know, a little of this, a little of that. Things like advising the First Lady on flatware and place settings for State dinners….."

"And what kind of weapon do you carry in this table setting consulting capacity of yours?"

"A Walther PPK .38, choosing China can sometimes be very dangerous work."

"And when was the last time you fired it?"

"A few hours ago actually, Ms. Windom and I were at the range."

"Beautiful family," Rose said as he turned away from the photo and sank back down into the little chair. He looked up at the ceiling, took a deep breath, then lowered his head and stared directly at Wilder. "Enough with the charades and smart ass comments Wilder. Cisco and his two goons were found murdered in the parking lot of the Tijuana Tavern around two this morning and I think you were involved."

"Listen detective, it's true I knew the guy and we weren't exactly close friends, but I really don't know anything about anyone being killed in some parking lot. Now, unless you have something more concrete to show me, Ms. Windom and I were just on our way out."

Once again Rose hefted his extra large body out of the chair and stood facing Jack. He handed him his business card. "That's fine Wilder, just don't leave town. We'll talk again real soon," he said as he brushed past Jack and headed for the door. "In the meantime, give me a call if you suddenly remember anything that might help keep you out of jail because it certainly looks like that's where you're headed."

"What the hell was that all about?" a very surprised Celeste said as she closed the door behind the corpulent detective.

"Long story" Jack said, "a very long complicated story."

Carmine sat low in his car down the block and watched as the detective climbed into his car and drove away.

Chapter 32

Jack's cell phone rang before he had the opportunity to explain everything to Celeste. "Jack, its Evant," said a tired voice on the other end of the line.

"Darrouzett," Jack said as he looked at his watch. "Don't you ever sleep? What time is it in Vienna?"

"Still early here Jack, only one in the morning. I've been at it for 12 hours, just getting my second wind. My boss gets cranky if I work less than 16 hours a day."

"So, what have you got for me?"

"Some pretty interesting stuff actually. We've been looking into every aspect of OPEC we can get our hands on. We talked to a few insiders from some of the OPEC member countries. As it turns out, a few of them tell us they were pressured to falsify some reports that were sent to the analysts at OPEC."

"What do you mean falsify?" Jack asked, as he sat back down and put his feet up on the coffee table.

"It looks like both the Saudis and the Venezuelans indicated that they had to cut their production by as much as 25 percent over the last six months or so. The truth is that they haven't cut production at all. They're just cranking out the crude and putting it into their reserves," Darrouzette replied. "And that's not all. Last week executives in the OPEC chain from both countries made a trip to the U.S. They arrived on March fourteenth, but we don't know where they went or why. We're still looking into it."

"Anything else?" Jack asked.

"Nothing else, yet."

"Okay, keep me posted. And Evant, thanks very much. I owe you big time for this one."

"Will do Jack," Evant said as he hung up.

"So, new developments in Vienna?" Celeste mused from across the room. Jack patted his hand on the couch next to him. Celeste sidled over and sat next to him. He put his arm around her and gave her a hug.

"A couple of leads to follow up on later, but nothing as important as what's going on here at the moment," Jack said. "That guy Lopeno and his two bodyguards were the ones who beat me up in the parking lot of the tavern that night I called you to come pick me up. I had a little chat with Lopeno and his guys sometime after that. They were hired by a guy named Bryson Chandler who happens to be the CEO of Global Oil, the company where both Garrison and Trini worked. By the time I was done, they realized the error of their ways and promised to behave. I also convinced Lopeno to ask around about Garrison's killing."

"That was crazy Jack. They beat you up once, they could have killed you. "

"Well, I am actually pretty good in close combat when I haven't had too much to drink, and I've found that a pool cue can be your best friend in a tough situation."

"What?"

"Never mind," Jack said. "What's important is this. I'm pretty sure that whoever killed Lopeno is going to come after me next. Lopeno was a loose end, and this guy thinks I'm one too."

"Oh my God Jack, you have to go to the police."

"In case you didn't notice, the police were just here and the good detective seems to think I'm the guy who killed Lopeno and his pals."

"So what are we going to do?"

Jack took a deep breath, turned to face Celeste and put a hand on each of her shoulders. He looked deep into her eyes and said, "There is no *we* in this, it's only me and the first thing I am going to do is get you out of here and someplace safe for a few days. I want you go pack a bag right now and drive across town and check into a hotel. I'll call you in a day or so."

"No way Jack Wilder," she said. "This is my apartment and I'm staying right here with you."

"Let me tell you something" he said. "For some reason, and I can't explain why, I care about you. I mean, I really care about you Celeste. If anything ever happened to you I would never forgive myself. You've got to believe me when I say I can take care of this. There are a lot of things you don't know about me, but know this. I have been in much, much worse situations and have come out without a scratch. There is really nothing for you to worry about. I can handle this, really I can."

After another half hour of arguing, Celeste finally gave in and reluctantly packed a bag and left.

Jack dialed his old pal Gordo Mansfield in Chicago. "Gordo," Jack said. "I have a favor to ask about our old friend Carmine Milano. Is there any way you can find out if he is still in Chicago? I need to find out quickly."

"Let me make a couple calls and I'll get right back to you."

Jack hung up and walked around the apartment making sure all the doors were locked and the shades pulled. He left a small opening in the front window to watch everything in the street with his night vision binoculars. He focused about two blocks down on the opposite side of the street. He was looking at a new white CTS Cadillac. He'd seen the car earlier in about the same spot and again in the parking lot at the shooting range.

Fifteen minutes later his phone rang. Jack answered without putting down the binoculars. "Jack, you must be psychic," Gordo said. "The guys over in the Organized Crime Unit tell me our guy got on a plane two days ago and headed for Houston. As far as they know he hasn't returned."

"Thanks Gordo. I still owe you."

"Jack, is there anything else I should know about what you're up to?"

"Not really, thanks again buddy, I'll be in touch." Jack hung up the phone and continued his surveillance.

One thing Carmine had learned in his years as a contract killer was patience. Patience was a key ingredient in the art of watching, stalking, planning and killing. He sat in the Caddy and watched as the lights in Celeste's apartment went dark. He waited another two hours, screwed the suppressor on the muzzle of his nine mil and got out of the car. He opened the trunk and removed the Houston PD uniform he had purchased earlier that day. He casually looked up and down the quiet street. The only sound to be heard was the buzzing of the street lights. Satisfied no one was watching he quickly changed into the uniform then strolled casually toward Celeste's apartment. Jack continued watching

Carmine with his night vision optics as the Italian approached.

As he walked he thought of his favorite Italian restaurant in downtown Chicago. He decided he'd have dinner there the next night on his way home from the airport. For some strange reason, he always craved a great Italian meal after a hit. Perhaps it came from the wonderful meals his mother had served him growing up on Chicago's South side. They didn't have much growing up. His alcoholic father had left them when Carmine was ten. Maybe his mother had tried to substitute his father's missing love by gorging him with homemade noodles and the great sauce that was forever simmering on the stove in their tiny apartment.

By the time he was 12 he was running numbers for the mob and supporting his mom. At age 16 he was packing a weapon. One late night he saw his father staggering out of a bar. He followed him into an alley and killed him without giving it a second thought. His future in the crime business had been solidified.

Chapter 33

Barry Godley stood up from his desk at CIA headquarters. He stretched his hands as high into the air as he could reach, then rocked up on his toes to stretch even higher. He had just spent the last seven hours looking at a computer screen correlating data on likely scenarios given various outcomes in an upcoming election in Pakistan. It was tedious work, researching data, reading files and typing up scenarios. He was glad to have it behind him. He sat back down and took a sip of the high octane energy drink. The corner of his desk was never without one.

Barry was the quintessential computer nerd if ever there were one. He wore a short sleeve plaid shirt that held a pocket protector stuffed with various colored pens and pencils. Pens and pencils he rarely used since his fingers spent most of their day on a keyboard. His thick, black rimmed glasses were tucked in under his long, unruly hair which framed a long acne scarred face with slightly oversized lips. His best feature, besides his incredible brain, was his eyes. He did have deep blue eyes that would be the envy of any movie star. He wore stained khaki pants that were too short for his thirty-three inch inseam. White socks and black shoes completed the look which lent credence to the "computer nerd" label he'd been given by his CIA associates long ago. "Barry the Wonder Boy," they called him. He was a strict vegan, a hair short of six feet tall and skinny as a rail.

Despite his geeky nerd appearance, Barry was no slouch when it came to the ladies. He had a serious girlfriend whom he had dated for the past three years. They met for lunch in the cafeteria every day. Friona Franklin and Barry Godley were true soul mates. She worked in another department as a computer analyst doing similar tasks.

The major difference between the two of them was that Friona wore a wrinkled white blouse instead of a plaid shirt, and she didn't have a pocket protector. Instead, she always had one or two pens or pencils perched somewhere in her overly abundant naturally curly red hair. She was never without her writing utensils. Her colleagues wondered if she took them out to shower. She was exactly the same height as Barry and always wore flat shoes so she wouldn't tower over the guy. She had a perfectly shaped face, not too round, not too long. Her emerald green eyes were accentuated by her smooth pearl white skin which was dotted with copious amounts of freckles. Barry often dreamt of playing connect the dots with those freckles starting somewhere around her small, firm breasts.

What to do next? Barry pondered as he looked over the many stacks of paper that covered his desk and the shelves in his cubicle. His gaze landed on a FedEx envelope tucked under a half dozen manila folders all marked Secret. "*Hmm,*" he said to himself as he pulled the envelope from beneath the folders. *This came in three days ago via overnight delivery. Must be important.* "Cool!" he said aloud as he looked at the package and saw it was from Jack Wilder. Jack was one of Barry's favorite people at the agency. While many of the spymasters made fun of him, Jack was always polite, considerate and expressed his gratitude when Barry did something for him.

Barry shoved several stacks of paper aside, ripped open the package and spread the contents on his desk. He gave a cursory glance to each document looking for a place to start. He saw memos from various OPEC oil ministers, copies of emails, phone logs, handwritten notes and receipts for wire transactions of money that had been sent to various accounts… lots of money.

Unable to find a suitable starting point he began to separate those items with dates into one stack and those without dates into another. Next he sorted those with dates chronologically hoping to establish a timeline of some kind. It looked like whatever the documents referred to had begun seven or eight months ago. Through it all, he really didn't know exactly what it was he was looking for. He just remembered Jack asking him to look over the data to see if he could make some sense of it.

Sifting through the documents he saw that most of them focused on oil production including output from specific oil wells in various oil producing countries. As all the documents were clearly related to oil, he made the logical jump to the current oil crisis facing the U.S. and other countries. It seemed like the only countries with oil surplus were the OPEC countries that produced it. Exports from those countries were down significantly, which meant they were either hoarding the oil or they weren't producing at previous levels for some reason, and the price of crude was rising out of site. Barry leaned back in his chair and stared at a spot high on the wall opposite his desk as various ideas and scenarios rattled around in his mind.

He leaned forward and smacked himself in the forehead with the palm of his hand. "Duh," he said out loud to no one in particular. He suddenly realized that several of the notes were on personal stationary for one Trinidad Palacios. The same Trinidad Palacios who worked for OPEC and was recently killed as he was about to begin a press conference.

Barry looked back through each document with renewed enthusiasm. He swiveled his chair to his keyboard and began a Google search. He typed in Venezuela oil production. Next he typed in worldwide oil production followed by worldwide oil consumption. As he read and gathered information he made notes. Worldwide oil production: 84.8 million barrels a day. Worldwide oil consumption: 89 million barrels a day. Proven oil reserves left in the world: 1.3 trillion barrels. Barry did some quick math. Sure, we're using more than we're producing, but 1.3 trillion barrels in reserves should last around forty years or more depending on usage and new production. *So why is there a shortage now?* The figures didn't tie to the current oil crisis that had caused prices to skyrocket. Barry did more research but couldn't find anything to indicate any concrete reasons for OPEC countries to reduce production. No matter how he looked at it, there was no indication the world was running short of oil.

He swiveled his chair again and took another look at the data Jack had sent. It was starting to make sense, the cables, money transfers and emails. Trini had somehow managed to figure it out. Barry couldn't tell who was behind it all, but he could tell that the oil shortage looked to be bogus. He leaned back and found his coveted spot on the wall to stare at. *The whole thing is a sham. There is no oil shortage. They made the whole thing up. That's what Palacios had discovered and he was about to tell the world about it. That's probably what got him killed.*

Barry picked up the phone and called Jack. "Jack, the whole thing is made up. It's a scam, a sham, a boondoggle of the highest magnitude dude and they're covering it all up."

"Whoa, Barry, slow down kid. What are you talking about?"

"I'm talking about the price of gas, man. The price of heating oil. The price of *everything* connected with the oil industry."

"And just how did you figure all this out?" Jack asked.

"Trinidad Palacios and Google," came the response. "It's all in the stuff you sent me. I think this guy Palacios had proof that these OPEC guys were behind the scam and that's probably why they offed him."

"Hang on Barry. Give me a little more."

"Ok, how's this," Barry said. "Palacios was looking at emails, wires, production reports, and money… always follow the money right? Somehow this Palacios dude saw huge transfers of money into key accounts. Bribery at its finest."

"Barry you are an underpaid genius for sure. Thanks a million. Let me know if anything else pops into that massive mind of yours."

"Will do JW," Barry said with a huge smile as he hung up the phone and reached for his energy drink.

Chapter 34

Carmine stood in front of the door to Celeste's apartment and rang the doorbell. Ballinger watched as Carmine approached the door. He was three blocks down in the opposite direction from where Carmine had parked. "Who's there?" Jack asked from behind the door as he looked through the peep hole.

"Houston Police Department, we got a report of a disturbance at this address," the hit man said as he casually surveyed the area.

"No disturbance here officer," Jack replied as he reached across his chest to remove the Walther from its holster. He lowered the weapon down, next to his right thigh.

"I can appreciate that sir, but we still need to come in and have a look around… department policy."

"Certainly officer, please come in," Jack said as he opened the door about halfway, crowding Carmine as he stepped into the room. Jack slammed the door against the Italian's right side knocking him off balance and into the wall of the entryway. Before Carmine could react, Jack hit him in the side of the head with the Walther, grabbed him by the back of the shirt, pulled him into the apartment and slammed his face against the entry wall.

"Hello Carmine, glad you could stop by" Jack said as he pushed the muzzle of the Walther into the back of Carmine's head, grabbing the Italian's gun with his free hand. He stuck the weapon in the back of his waist band. "Hands behind your back, don't make me say it twice." Jack took a pair of plasticuffs out of his pocked and snapped them on the killer's wrists.

Carmine never had a chance to even think about where he went wrong. It was clear Wilder was expecting him. This was something he hadn't planned for at all.

Jack marched him into the middle of the living room and kicked his feet out from under him. Carmine collapsed into the kitchen chair Jack had brought in for the occasion. Wilder put the Walther back in his holster and laid Carmine's nine mil on the coffee table next to a roll of duct tape. Jack pulled on a pair of latex gloves, picked up the tape and slowly walked in circles around Carmine wrapping him and the chair with it until he had used up about half the roll.

"So, Mr. Milano, you have been a very busy boy. We have a lot to talk about," Jack said as he continued applying the duct tape. "Tell me about Garrison Shepherd." Carmine jerked first left, then right thinking he could tear the tape. No such luck.

"The name doesn't ring a bell," Carmine said. "You must have me confused with someone else. I am a police officer with the Houston Police Department and you are in a lot of trouble." Carmine eyed the gun on the coffee table trying to figure a way to get to it.

"So, tell me Mr. Houston Police Department officer, when did the department start issuing Hertz rental cars to beat cops? And why do you keep your uniform in the trunk of the rented car?" Carmine seemed to look past Jack as he was being questioned. He furrowed his brow trying to figure out what was going on and who the guy was that had quietly slipped into the room behind Jack.

Jack saw Carmine's puzzled look and sensed someone behind him. He started to turn, but it was too late. Ballinger hit him in the back of the head with a leather covered sap. Jack's knees buckled and he fell to the floor, out like a light. Without a word, Ballinger picked the nine mil off the coffee table, pointed it at Carmine and shot him once in the head. He smoothly took a handkerchief out of his pocket and carefully wiped the weapon clean. Then he firmly placed the gun in Jack's hand. He took one quick look around the room and left through the front door as quietly as he had come in. the blood pooled in Carmine's lap as his head hung limp, his body still taped to the chair.

Jack opened his eyes, but they didn't focus. He could see the outline of someone hovering over him. He thought the person was saying his name, but wasn't sure. He had a tremendous headache and was trying to make sense of what had happened. His vision finally cleared enough for him to see that it was Celeste down on her knees next to him calling his name. "Jack, are you okay? What happened? Who is the guy in the chair? Whose gun is this?" Celeste seemed to be repeating those same questions over and over.

Jack thought he could hear sirens in the background. *Had someone called an ambulance for him?* Then it all came flooding back to him at once. The guy in the chair was Carmine Milano. He didn't know exactly what had happened, but he had a pretty good idea. No he was definitely not okay.

"Gun, what gun?" Jack asked as he tried to sit up. Celeste held her hand on his chest, keeping him down. Jack's focus was now pretty clear. He looked at the chair in the middle of the room which held a very dead Carmine Milano.

"Lie still," she said. "You were unconscious when I got here a few minutes ago. I got worried about you and came back. Looks like a lot happened while I was gone." The sirens grew louder.

"Show me the gun," Jack said. Celeste picked up the suppressed nine mil that had been in Jack's hand and gave it to him. "Get me something I can use to wipe my prints off this thing,   hurry," Jack said. Celeste ran into the kitchen and returned with a dish towel and some ice. Jack was sitting up, dizzy and still hurting like hell, but sitting up nonetheless. He took the towel from Celeste and quickly wiped Milano's gun clean before laying it back down on the floor. Celeste took the towel back, wrapped some ice in it and applied it to the huge lump growing on back of Jack's aching head.

Jack felt like his head was going to explode from the piercing wail of the sirens as they pulled up in front of the apartment. The pain was made worse by the pounding on the front door.

"Houston Police, open the door!" Celeste rose quickly and opened the door as two police officers charged in with their weapons drawn. "Miss, please stay right where you are and keep your hands out where we can see them," said the first officer. Celeste let the ice and towel drop to the floor. The second officer pointed his weapon at Jack and said, "Sir, please place your hands behind your head and don't attempt to move." Jack was happy to comply. Holding his hands behind his head seemed to help the throbbing, although he could feel something wet and sticky against his interlaced fingers. Celeste stood frozen, barely breathing, trying to figure out what was going on and why there was a dead guy duct taped to a kitchen chair in her living room.

One of the officers walked over to the deceased hit man and felt his neck for a pulse, knowing he wouldn't find one. Then he walked over to Jack, holstered his weapon and pulled Jack's hands away from his head one at a time and placed them in handcuffs behind his back. He then helped Jack stand

and walked him over to the couch. Jack sat on the couch and listened to the radio chatter as the police officer reported to his dispatcher. The scene was secure with two suspects in custody and they needed a homicide detective as soon as possible.

The first officer turned Celeste around and cuffed her as well, then took her into the bedroom and closed the door so Jack couldn't hear what was being said. He asked her to explain exactly what had happened. Celeste told him she had been out late and had come home to find the front door unlocked. She had come inside and found everything and everyone exactly as it looked. There was one unconscious boyfriend on the floor and one dead guy taped to a chair. Jack told essentially the same story. He had come in late, found a dead guy taped to a chair and was hit from behind and rendered unconscious.

A short time later the generously proportioned detective Rose arrived once again. He instructed one officer to stay at the front door and to start logging everyone in and out. He looked at Jack and said "Well Jack old buddy, looks like you and your lady friend here have really stepped in it this time. You seem to be some kind of killing machine. First Cisco and his buddies, now this guy in the chair." Rose once again walked around the room carefully taking everything in as he walked. "So, tell me," he said as he turned to face Jack, "who is the dead guy in the chair and how is it that he came to be taped to the chair.

"You know about as much as I know," Jack said. "I never saw the guy before tonight."

"Oh, I doubt that very much Jack. I think you know more than you're telling me, much more."

"Think whatever you like detective. I believe that's what the good citizens of Houston pay you to do."

Another set of flashing red lights arrived as the Crime Scene Investigation unit arrived. Two CSI techs stopped at the door, gave their names to the officer who dutifully entered them into the log, then came into the room. "Don't you just love being called out in the middle of the night," Rose said dryly as he looked at the two techs. "Bag and print the nine millimeter on the floor. Do the same with Mr. Wilder's Walther PPK and check both weapons to see if they were recently fired. Print both suspects and check them for gunshot residue. When you're done with that, check the duct tape for prints, print the dead guy, and try and figure out just who he is, or was."

When Jack heard the detective tell the tech to check the duct tape for prints he was glad he had worn gloves while gift wrapping Carmine. He'd pulled them off and tossed them in the trash before starting to question the thug. He also knew that no GSR would be found on him or Celeste and, of course, he'd wiped his prints off Carmine's gun. Add to that the lump the size of Cleveland on the back of his head and anything the good detective had was barely circumstantial at best.

"How long has Mr. Duct Tape here been dead" Rose asked one of the CSI techs as he nodded his head toward Carmine.

"Looks like about an hour, give or take," the tech replied. Rose made a note on the small writing tablet he held in his hand.

"And what about GSR on these two?" Rose said pointing at Jack and Celeste.

"Negative" the tech replied. "Doesn't look like either one of them have fired a gun tonight.

"And what about the dead guy's cause of death?"

"Well detective, I'm gonna go out on a limb here and say it probably has something to do with the bullet hole in the middle of his forehead. Looks like a nine millimeter, same as the weapon we found on the floor."

"Great, another smart ass," Rose said as he turned back to Jack and Celeste. "Time for you both to leave. I don't care where you go, just get your sorry butts out of my crime scene. Don't leave town and be sure and make yourselves available for the next few days. I'm going to have more questions for you later." With that he motioned to one of the officers who removed the handcuffs from Jack and Celeste.

"Can I at least pack a bag?" Celeste asked.

"The answer to that would be a no," Rose replied. His turn to be a smart ass. "You can't pack a bag and you can't touch anything. Just leave. We'll let you know when you can have your apartment back." Celeste snagged her purse off the hook by the front door on the way out. No one noticed her take it.

Jack and Celeste checked into a Holiday Inn Express. As they walked through the lobby Jack picked up a complimentary copy of the Houston Chronicle. The headline on page one caught his eye. *Global Oil CEO dies in car crash.* After they reached their room Jack sat down at the table and read the rest of the story.

"What are you reading?"

"Something odd," Jack replied. "Bryson Chandler, the guy who hired Cisco to rough me up, was killed in a car crash yesterday. He was a guest at the Montana ranch of some Senator. The article says he lost control of his car on a steep hill after leaving the Senator's ranch. Alcohol was believed to have been a factor in the accident. I was going to have another talk with him, but haven't had the time. He certainly won't be answering my questions now."

"Well, what's next then?" Celeste said, as she lay back on the bed and kicked off her shoes.

"Well, next, I'm going to go to bed and get some sleep. Then, first thing in the morning I'm going to pay a visit to the widow Shepherd. There's got to be some kind of connection with her somehow. She knows something. Garrison and Trini both worked at Global Oil, they're both dead. The CEO of Global dies in a car accident. It doesn't add up."

He kissed her gently on the forehead and rolled over on the bed. It wasn't long before he was sleeping like a baby.

Celeste picked up the television remote and clicked it on. A late night rerun of Wheel of Fortune blasted into the room. She immediately hit the mute button on the remote. Didn't want to interrupt Jack's beauty sleep. Someone had just asked Pat Sajack for an L. "Love It or Leave It," Celeste said quietly. "That's the answer, Love It or Leave It." She fell back onto the pillow and stared at the ceiling. She recapped the day in her mind. Let's see, came home to find my boyfriend out cold on the floor. Found a dead guy taped to a chair in my living room. I was nearly arrested. I was handcuffed and taken into the bedroom. Got kicked out of my apartment and now living in a Holiday Inn. Just another average day with Jack Wilder. Two minutes later she was snoring. Somehow she always found it easier to sleep with the TV on.

Chapter 35

On the way over to Angelina's the next morning, Jack called Donna Crowley, Bryson Chandler's administrative assistant. "Donna, Jack Wilder here. I just read about Chandler. What happened?"

"I can't say for sure Jack. All we know is what we read in the paper. The only thing I can say for sure is that there doesn't seem to be too many tears being shed here. The paper said alcohol may have been a factor. That's not surprising; the guy drank like a fish."

"Okay," Jack said, "please give me a call if you hear anything more."

Jack didn't bother to ring the bell at Angelina Shepherd's home. He just pounded on the door pretending it was her head. He wanted to get as much aggression out of his system as he could before he started to have an actual conversation with the woman.

"Jack, I wasn't expecting you," Angelina said as she opened the door. "You should have called, I was just going out."

"Really," he replied dead pan. "I would expect you to have your purse and keys in your hand if you were on your way out."

"I was, uh, just headed into the bedroom to get them when you knocked. Or should I say pounded on the door. What do you want Jack?"

"What I want," Jack said, "is some truthful answers from you about Garrison and about your former husband."

"I don't have to talk to you about any of that Jack," she replied, as she tried to close the door. She was too slow. Jack's foot was already between the door and the door frame. He pushed the door back nearly knocking her over as he marched into the room.

"We can do this the easy way or the hard way," he said, as he turned to face her. "Which is it going to be?"

"Get out or I'm calling the police!" She pulled her cell phone out of her pocket and began to punch in a number.

Jack grabbed the phone from her hand, dropped it to the marble floor and stomped on it with his heel. The latest and most expensive smart phone on the market shattered as parts flew in every direction. Once again Jack said "The easy way or the hard way Ange, which is it going to be?"

"You're a no good SOB!" Angie screamed. "I don't know how Garrison could have ever been friends with a monster like you."

"The feeling is mutual Missy, and you really have no idea who Garrison Shepherd really was."

Not true, I loved him deeply."

"I doubt that."

"So Jack, just ask me whatever it is you want to know and get the hell out of my house."

Jack stopped for a few seconds and stared at the woman. She was clearly angry, but showed none of the emotion she should have for someone who recently lost a husband.

For starters, where were you when Garrison was killed?"

"I was out shopping. That's something I already told the police."

"Yes, but they weren't able to confirm that."

"Not my problem. Next question"

"Who is Carmine Milano?" Jack noticed a slight movement of Angelina's eyes as she glanced left and quickly looked back at him. It was a nearly imperceptive movement, just enough to tell Jack that her answer was going to be a lie.

"Never heard of him."

"How much did you pay him to kill Garrison?" No movement of the eyes this time.

"I have no idea what you're talking about."

"How much did you pay him to kill Bardwell Bishop?" There it was again, the glancing away then looking back. The eyes never lie.

"I didn't pay anybody to kill Bardwell," Angelina said as she took a step toward Jack. "I think I've answered enough of your ridiculous questions. Now get out of my house!"

"Yes you have," Jack said. "Yes, you have." He turned and walked out the front door.

"*That bastard*," Angelina said to herself as she slammed the door behind Jack. She hadn't hesitated when she pulled the trigger five times to kill Garrison and she wouldn't hesitate to do it again with Jack in her sights. She had never liked him. She decided to kill Garrison herself after Carmine turned her down, and she could certainly kill again if she felt the need. Carmine had other pressing matters to attend to he'd said. He should have been anxious to do another job for her after the fortune she'd paid him to kill Bardwell. Maybe his other stuff was done and she could have him kill Jack. Some things are better left to professionals. She picked up the phone and dialed his number, got an answering machine and left a message for him to call her.

Jack sat in his car and thought about what she'd said. He was sure she was lying about not knowing Milano and had probably paid him to kill Bardwell Bishop. On the other hand, he didn't think she hired Milano to kill Garrison. The homicide detective had said that Garrison was shot five times in the back. That's sloppy work and way below Milano's expertise. If it had been him, there would have been only one shot.

Jack thought more about it. Could it have been Cisco that killed Garrison? Probably not, he thought, Cisco was a thug who liked to beat people up for money in between drug deals. He didn't seem like the type who actually had the guts to pull a trigger. Still, for the right amount of money, anything was possible. Could it have been the same guy who killed Trini Palacios? Again, too sloppy, Jack thought to himself. A sniper with that kind of expertise would have used only one bullet and would have been hundreds of yards away.

As Jack turned these things over and over in his mind he concluded that it had to have been some other thug, one slightly above Cisco's level. Maybe someone who hadn't done it before and was slightly panicked, hence the overkill with five shots. An amateur who wanted to make sure the job got done. Then it hit him like a ton of bricks, Angelina! Could she have been the one who killed Garrison? He decided he needed to take a closer look around her house. Jack started the car and drove back to the motel to pick up Celeste. The least he could do was take her out to a nice dinner somewhere. He had a lot of explaining to do.

When he arrived back at the motel, the smell of gun oil met him at the door. He found Celeste sitting at the small table with a rag, his Glock 26 in pieces, a container of gun oil and a six pack of Shiner.

"What are you up to?" Jack asked.

"Cleaning your Glock." I went to the shooting range after you left. The guy behind the counter showed me how to do it and sold me everything I needed. I shot fifty rounds and hit dead center eight out of 10 times."

Celeste finished assembling the weapon, laid it on the table and took a sip of beer. "And now Jack Wilder, you have a lot of explaining to do, starting with the dead guy in my apartment." Jack opened a bottle for himself and sat down on the end of the bed. Her tone reminded him of being scolded by his mother when he was a teenager.

"Hmm…where to start," he said.

"Well at the beginning of course."

Jack took another sip of beer and began his long explanation of recent events starting with his conversation with Angelina. He told Celeste he thought Angelina was clearly lying about how her first husband died. He explained his relationship with

Cisco and how he had warned Cisco to leave town. He expressed his doubts to Celeste about Garrison being killed by a professional. He told her about his phone call to Gordo in Chicago and the fact that Carmine Milano had probably been hired by Angelina to kill her first husband. Lastly, he told her again that when Cisco and his pals had been killed, he figured whoever did it was cleaning up loose ends and would probably come after him. His suspicions were confirmed when Milano showed up at Celeste's apartment. The only thing he didn't know, he told her, was who had whacked him in the back of the head and killed Milano.

Chapter 36

After leaving Jack unconscious on the floor and dispatching Carmine Milano, Ballinger quietly left Celeste's apartment. On his way to the airport in the thick Houston traffic he called the Senator.

"I think we can put Wilder on the back burner for a while. He's going to be busy trying to explain a dead gentleman duct taped to a chair in his girlfriend's apartment. I believe the gun that killed the guy has Wilder's prints all over it."

"Ah, yes, I see," the Senator said as he signed a document handed to him by his secretary and handed it back to her. When she closed the office door behind her he said to Ballinger, "just who was the guy in the chair?" Ballinger leaned on the horn as a car in the next lane signaled right and turned left into his lane.

"Don't know, don't care," Ballinger replied. "My guess is that he was someone Wilder was about to have a pretty serious conversation with about something. I just made the best of the opportunity that presented itself. The fellow showed up while I was watching the apartment." Ballinger leaned on the horn again, "Texas moron!" he shouted to the oblivious driver who had just crossed over two lanes of traffic and cut him off. "I swear, if I have to spend one more day in this state I'm gonna kill myself about a hundred Texans. Anyway, I saw this guy take the cop uniform out of the trunk of his car, obviously not a real cop and obviously not the brightest bulb in the pack, seeing as how he ended up being duct taped to a chair."

Kingsbury opened the expensive wooden humidor on his desk, took out a Cuban cigar, clipped the tip and lit it. "Well done my friend," he said as he leaned back in his chair, smiled and blew a puff of smoke towards the ceiling. "Well done indeed. When this is all done I'm thinking you should probably get a bonus of some kind. In the meantime, I'll have the usual amount wired to your account in the Bahamas. I'll see you back at the ranch next week."

Kingsbury called one of his top lieutenants into his office. "Go through the usual channels and start hinting that I'm about to announce my candidacy for President. Let it be known that I am very seriously concerned about the oil shortage and this President's lack of action on such a critical issue." Two hours later Kingsbury got a call from a Washington Post reporter. "Senator, this is Kyle Hudson from the Washington Post. Is it true that you think the President is floundering in his handling of the oil crisis? What are your thoughts on how it should be handled? Are you going to be running for President?"

"Well Kyle, I don't ordinarily take calls direct from reporters. I prefer they call my secretary and set up a meeting, but I will make an exception in this case and only if it is off the record."

"If that's the way it has to be I'll take anything I can get as long as I can say an un-named source in the Senator's office."

"If that will help you with what you're looking for, that will be fine." Kingsbury leaned a little further back in his chair and took another puff of his expensive Cuban cigar.

"So, is it true that you think the President is floundering in his handling of the oil crisis?"

"Well, given my position as Chair of the Committee on Energy and Natural Resources, I think I may have a little more insight into the situation than the President does, and given his lack of experience in energy issues, I think he may be in a little over his head."

"Would you care to elaborate on that?"

"Only to say that the President's record on the U.S. energy policies speaks for itself. And given that he is now a lame duck, well, I think he's stalling to make it someone else's problem.

"Okay, let's change the subject. Is there any truth to the rumor that you are going to run for President?"

"Now Mr. Hudson, you have hit the proverbial gold mine. I will give you the scoop on that issue and you can run with it. Yes, I will formally announce my candidacy later this week. And now I'm afraid I have another important call coming in that I must take. If you want to talk further, call my secretary and make an appointment to come in and see me."

Kingsbury hung up the phone and called Leroy Marshall, his Vice Chair of the Committee on Energy and Natural Resources. Leroy was a mousy little man of moderate stature who wore thick glasses and spoke with a slight lisp. His suits fit him poorly and always looked like he'd slept in them. He'd been in the Senate for close to 20 years without ever having a serious challenger in his home district. Despite his awkward appearance, he was well liked by his constituency back in Minnesota and was a genius at numbers, especially numbers that related to energy. He despised nicknames and always insisted that his staff and everyone around him refer to him by his given name of Leroy, not Lee, but Leroy. Like most of the others on the committee, he knew the power of Kingsbury and his ability to destroy those who got in his way.

"Lee, I'm announcing my candidacy for President tomorrow. I'm going to use the President's handling of the oil shortage as my springboard. I am essentially going to say the President is full of crap and doesn't know what he is doing, and I expect you to be there with me. I want you to come up with some number mumbo jumbo about oil production that will support what I'm saying about the President."

"Sure," Marshall said, "I would be happy to."

Kingsbury hung up the phone and rubbed his hands together. He looked at himself in the mirror on the wall next to the door in his office and smiled. *Now the real fun begins and there's no way I can lose.*

Chapter 37

After two nights in a motel, Jack and Celeste were allowed back in her apartment. They'd decided to take a break from everything and spent two days just lying around the pool relaxing and drinking Margaritas. Now sitting at the kitchen table, Jack felt recharged and ready to go. He was thinking about what his next step would be when his phone rang. It was Evant. "Jack, I have a little more information for you about the meeting all the oil executives went to in the U.S. in the middle of March. After a little digging and beating a few guys with a rubber hose, we found out that they were meeting at a ranch somewhere in Montana, wherever that is. Apparently the ranch belongs to some U.S. Senator."

"You really beat guys with a hose to get information?"

"Just kidding Jack, there are no beatings with rubber hoses anymore. We actually use electric shock. It's amazing the information you can get from people with a couple hundred volts of electricity. A hundred and ten volts gets their attention and you can get anything you want when you crank it up to two hundred."

Jack hung up the phone wondering if Evant and his crew really did shock people into giving them the information they wanted. *Surely he didn't. But then again?*

Jack made a quick call to Barry the Wonder Boy and asked him to find out who the U.S. Senator was that owned a ranch in Montana. "Hold on a sec," Barry said. Jack could hear the clicking of fingers on a keyboard interrupted once by the slurping of some kind of drink. A dozen or so keystrokes later Barry came back "Kid stuff," he said. "Your guy is none other than Hamilton Kingsbury III, Republican Senator from the great state of Texas. He was a two term congressman then moved up to the senate. A Yale MBA dripping with money, mostly from oil and he's chairman of the Committee on Energy and Natural Resources."

"Thanks Barry. Like I said, you're an underpaid genius. Do me a favor and see what else you can dig up on the good Senator and get back to me as soon as you can."

Jack leaned back in his chair put his thumb on his chin and tapped his upper lip with his forefinger. He was deep in thought wondering about the meeting in Montana when Celeste called. "I'm just finishing up at the shooting range," she said. "Hit the target eight out of eight with my last round."

"I've created a monster, a crazed out of control pistol packing mama with an itchy trigger finger" he replied. "Just remember, shooting paper targets is a whole lot different than shooting living, breathing people. Let's hope you never have to do that."

"You're right as usual," she replied. "Anything new on the dead guy in our apartment?"

"Haven't heard a thing."

"Okay I'm on my way, see you in about a half hour."

Hmm... our apartment? He had been there quite a while and was certainly feeling at home. Once again he wondered just where this relationship was headed.

Jack quickly put those thoughts on the back burner when Barry the Wonder Boy called back.

"Okay, JW, here's the scoop. The good Senator was born with the proverbial silver spoon in his mouth, only in his case it wasn't silver it was pure gold and I'm talking gold with a capital G. He's worth somewhere around a gazillion dollars. Always had the finest of everything, the best and most prestigious private schools. Daddy died and left him about a half a gazillion dollars which he parlayed into the full gazillion. Shortly after the old man died he parked his mom in a nursing home. Only visited her once in the entire time she was there and that was to get her signature on some legal document."

Barry paused to take a quick sip of his high octane energy drink. Jack could hear the slurp over the phone."Ah, love that stuff," Barry said as he took up where he left off. "It seems the good Senator has a well deserved reputation for being ruthless and leaving a lot of bodies in his wake. That is to say bodies in the metaphoric sense, although there may be some real ones buried out there somewhere." Another even bigger sip of energy drink. Wonder Boy was wound up and on a roll. "And then there's the ranch," he said as he let out a deep breath and squelched a burp. "The ranch is like Fort Knox with security better than what the secret service offers you know who. I'm talking about Mr. Lame Duck in the big White House down on the corner."

"Okay Barry, take another breath. Slow down a bit there, Speedy. You're about to explode."

"Oh, yeah, right, must be the energy drink. I love that stuff. Did I already say that?"

"Must be, so what else have you got?"

"That's about it so far. If you want I can probably hack his computer system at the ranch or even at his senate office, or both. Just say the word and I'm on it like white on rice."

"I'll have to think about that one," Jack said.

"Now, here's what I want you to do, Barry. Dump the rest of that energy drink down the sink, go outside and spend a half hour or so walking around the compound before you do explode. Then go back inside and do some more digging on the Senator. See if you can find out who is on his staff and what their backgrounds are. Also, see if you can find out what his committee is working on, especially anything that may have to do with the oil shortage. See if you can get a hold of his calendar somehow. I'd like to know who he's seen and why."

"Okay dude, whatever you say. Dump the drink, go for a walk and dig up some more stuff on daddy big bucks, got it." And with that Barry was gone, hopefully to walk around the compound as Jack suggested. He really did sound like he was about to explode.

Chapter 38

Celeste arrived home with a six pack of Shiner in hand. "Nothing like a good bottle of beer after a hard day at the shooting range killing paper people."

"Yup, you gotta watch out for those paper people, they can be a real terror. I think I saw one lurking out by the pool earlier today. Turned out to be nothing but a hot babe in a paper thin bikini," Jack replied.

Celeste smacked him on the arm. "In your dreams" she said. "So, anything new on the late Mr. Milano?"

"No, but I did find out some interesting things about the oil shortage. It seems several OPEC oil execs were meeting at a Senator's ranch in Montana. Some guy named Kingsbury. Hamilton Kingsbury III, to be precise. And here's another thing. Remember that guy Chandler from Global Oil killed in the car accident? Well, he was leaving Kingsbury's ranch when he had his accident."

"I've heard of Kingsbury," she replied. "He's a very wealthy Senator from Texas, been in the news a lot. There seems to be a lot of posturing going on. I'm betting he's gonna make a run at the White House. Every time I've seen him on TV he's talking trash about the President and the way he's handling the oil shortage. I think he's chairman of some critical committee."

"You're probably right," Jack said as he popped the top off a Shiner. "What I would like to know is why he was meeting with all those oil people at his ranch and why there was nothing about it in the news. You would think an event like that would get big coverage, especially with this oil thing going on. And, the article about Bryson Chandler and the car wreck didn't mention that there were foreign oil executives at a meeting at the ranch. In fact, the article just said he was vacationing at the Kingsbury ranch. Reporters just don't seem to dig around for all the dirt like they did in the days of Woodward and Bernstein. Guess I'm gonna have to do it myself." He took a sip of beer, stared out the window for a few seconds then said "and the other thing I'm going to have to do myself is have a look around Angelina Shepherd's house when she's not there."

Jack parked his car several blocks up the street from the Shepherd house and patiently watched the front door with his binoculars. It was just after six a.m. He lowered the binoculars and took a bite of an apple fritter he'd picked up at a donut shop on the way. He followed the bite with a sip of hot coffee. The door opened and Angelina left wearing workout clothes and carrying her gym bag. The only thing she worked harder at than stealing other people's money was keeping herself fit and beautiful. "*Time to go to work*," He poured what was left of the coffee into the street as he opened the car door and headed to the house.

After looking around for nosey neighbors, he walked up to the front door like he owned the place. He discretely used his lock pick set and had the door open in less than a minute and he was in. There was no alarm to disarm. He had noticed that on his earlier visit. The upscale Houston neighborhood was packed with tastefully landscaped yards kept up by hired help, most of whom didn't speak English. People in those kinds of neighborhoods don't push lawn mowers or pull weeds as long as there is money to have someone else do it. If a bus from Immigration and Naturalization Service ever showed up in the neighborhood there would be flower beds full of weeds and uncut lawns. The people would have to take care of their yards themselves.

The house itself was only minimally ostentatious. It was a contemporary, two story affair with a brick facade that ran all the way up and around the entry. The entry itself was highlighted by a huge modern window the height of the entire second story, tastefully set above the two ornate, custom made oak front doors. A chandelier the size of Cleveland hung from the ceiling and could be seen through the giant window from a block away. An oversized three car garage sat off to the left of the house. A covered arched walkway joined the two structures.

Jack stood in the huge marble-floored entry trying to decide where to start. Off to the right was a formal living room furnished with white leather couches sitting on a light tan, deep plush, carpet. The room looked like a showcase that no one had ever set foot in. Straight ahead was a great room with a luxury kitchen off to the right. It was the kind of kitchen any chef would kill for. To the left, opposite the formal living room and behind two walnut framed glass doors was a study.

After a quick walkthrough of the entire house to be sure he was alone, Jack headed back to the study. The room had floor to ceiling book shelves on two walls. They held a variety of books, mostly for show, and several original, expensive Remington bronze sculptures. The centerpiece of the room was an expensive, oversized walnut and teak executive desk which sat in front of a matching credenza. Jack put on a pair of latex gloves and opened each of the desk drawers, surveying the contents. On one corner of the credenza was a picture of a bikini clad Angelina reclining in a cabana lounge chair sipping what looked like a Mai-Tai. The building in the background looked to be the Hualalai Four Seasons in Hawaii. A search of the shelves and drawers of the credenza turned up nothing of note.

Jack turned his attention to the desk. In the first drawer he found nothing but the usual assortment of paper, pens, paperclips and other desk junk most people keep in their desks. The second drawer contained a stack of paper held together by a giant black clip. It also held the usual kind of stuff people keep; utility bills, credit card receipts and so forth. Jack's eyes were drawn to a car rental receipt for a Mercedes. It was dated the same day in March that Garrison had been killed. Jack remembered Detective

Bonham mentioning that a witness had seen a black Mercedes in the area where Garrison was jogging on the day he was killed. Jack carefully closed the two doors and headed for the Great Room.

The cavernous space was clearly the center of the house where most things happened. A solid oak wet bar took up one of the huge corners and a river rock fireplace stood at the opposite corner. The largest wall held the biggest flat screen television Jack had ever seen with about 10 expensive Bose speakers discretely placed around it as well as in each corner of the room. A giant leather couch and two matching recliners were carefully placed for maximum viewing of the giant screen. Several Tiffany lamps tastefully accented the huge space. The corner opposite the fireplace had a reading nook with tall bookcases located on either side of yet another expensive leather recliner.

As Jack walked through the great room and up the stairs he couldn't help but notice how sterile the whole place felt. The house had obviously been decorated by a professional, yet it seemed more like a model home, not a home where anyone lived.

The master suite was in keeping with the rest of the house, totally immaculate. Jack got on his knees and looked under the king size bed first, nothing there but a few dust bunnies that had somehow managed to escape the long arm of the housekeeper. There was a reading chair sitting in the corner. A tall brass lamp stood guard over the trashy romance novel lying open on the small table next to the chair. Another trashy romance novel by the same author sat on the end table next to the huge, neatly made up bed.

Jack took one last look around the big bedroom and headed for the expansive walk-in closet. The closet seemed nearly as big as Celeste's entire apartment. Jack took a deep breath and wondered if the bitch had Garrison living way beyond his means. Like the study, there were floor to ceiling shelves around the perimeter. The center held several racks of clothing. Not one single men's item was visible. Angelina had wasted no time totally erasing Garrison from her life. Most of the shelves held shoe boxes. Jack picked up and inspected the first five shoe boxes, quickly getting a feel for how much a pair of women's shoes weighed. He didn't open the next five boxes, he could tell by the weight they didn't contain what he was looking for.

Then he found it as he picked up the eleventh box; it was heavier than the rest. He opened the box and there it was, a brand new Glock 26 along with five brass casings. Jack popped the 10 round magazine out of the nine millimeter and counted the number of rounds... five in the clip and none in the chamber. Garrison had been hit five times. Jack wondered why the fool woman would bother to keep the gun. Most people would have tossed it somewhere in the Gulf, or at the least, buried it somewhere.

Jack replaced the magazine and put the gun back in the shoebox just as he had found it. He took out his cell phone and took two quick pictures of the gun in the box, replaced the lid and took a picture of the outside of the box. The box originally held a pair of size six black Jimmy Choo platforms. He carefully put everything back on the shelf exactly as he had found it. He was tempted to take it with him, but he knew he couldn't be the one to find it. He had no warrant and had broken into the house. None of it even close to acceptable in a courtroom. It had to be found by the police. The big issue was coming up with probable cause for the police to search the house.

Jack was in a quandary when he left Angelina's house. He was sure the gun he had found was the same one that had killed Garrison and that Angelina's prints would be the only ones found on the gun. What he still couldn't see was the connection to the death of Trini Palacios. Maybe there wasn't one. He spent most of the time driving back to Celeste's thinking of ways to kill Angelina. He knew he wouldn't, but he couldn't help thinking about it. He had killed lots of people all over the world, but they had all committed crimes much worse than Angelina and with a lot more at stake. No, he couldn't kill her. He needed to get her indicted and tried for Garrison's murder. He just had to figure out how to do it.

Chapter 39

Jack ran it all through his mind once more as he drove. He just couldn't see any connection between the two murders. The logical next step would be to find out more info on what the powerful Senator was up to. He knew he'd never be able to get an appointment to see the guy, so he'd do the next best thing. He would drop in on old Hamilton in person. He called Celeste and told her he wouldn't be home that night. *Home*, now even *he* was thinking of it as their place. He drove straight to the airport and got on the next flight to Washington DC. He called Langley and arranged for Barry the Wonder Boy to pick him up at Reagan International just after midnight.

As they drove to Jack's apartment in Alexandria, Barry filled him in on what he'd found out about the Senator. "Nearly everything at the Senator's ranch is computerized," Barry said. "And of course they have Wi-Fi and some pretty sophisticated firewalls, but only sophisticated for ordinary computer geeks who don't have the superb skills I possess. I'm so good it's almost scary. Cracking their system was easy." Raindrops began to pelt the windshield. Jack looked out the window, up at the sky, nothing but heavy black clouds in every direction. He had hoped to go for a run later. He hated running in the rain. He needed to clear the cobwebs out of his head and running always seemed to help.

"I was able to hack into the system and see the guest list for all the ranch visitors," Barry continued.

"On the days you asked about there were some guys with funny names from Venezuela, Saudi Arabia and a few others from the Middle East. There was also a group of ladies with names like Bunny and Charity with addresses in Las Vegas, Nevada. Ladies with similar names and addresses also visited on several other occasions. I'm thinking party girls to provide entertainment for the guests."

Barry went from 40 mph to zero as he skidded to a stop at a red light. He had been trying to will it to change with his mind. It didn't work.

"So what else did you learn?" Jack asked as he dug his fingers and palms out of the soft dashboard of Barry's car. Even with Barry's poor driving skills, the ride was far better than some of the crazy cab rides he'd taken in some foreign countries.

"Well, there's this guy who signs in and out with the letter B. No name, just the letter B. I couldn't find anything about him. Just B, maybe B for Bad Ass. The only other thing is the committee the Senator chairs. I couldn't find out what they are up to, but they are a powerful committee with a lot of control over energy policies in this country. I'm sure the Senator has a front row seat on anything and everything having to do with the oil shortage stuff."

"Okay," Jack said as he got out of the car and held his hand up to his forehead to shield the heavy rain from his eyes. "Thanks, and thanks for the lift. Keep digging and let me know if you come up with anything else."

The rain began to let up a little bit but not enough for a run, probably not a good idea to run at one-thirty in the morning anyway. He opened the door to his sparse apartment and was immediately met by Angus who first growled, then purred and rubbed himself against Jack's legs as they both walked into the kitchen. Jack nearly tripped as Angus wove in and out of his legs, meowing and growling in turns. He'd never been cussed out by cat, but he thought this must be close. Much to the cat's dismay, Mrs. Dickenson was apparently quite the miser when it came to sharing a beer or two.

Jack looked at his watch, nearly two a.m. Nothing more to get done at this hour. He got himself a beer, poured about a third of it into the cat's dish, put his feet up on the coffee table and turned on the TV. A replay of the nightly news was on. The lead story was the announcement of Hamilton Kingsbury declaring his run for the presidency. There was a short clip of the Senator bashing the President's poor handling of the oil crisis. Jack knew Barry hadn't had time to get home yet. He called the Wonder Boy's cell phone..

"Barry, what can you tell me about the Senator's daily routine?"

"He usually hits the Senate's private gym around five-thirty each morning, works out for an hour then heads to the Starbucks on Pennsylvania Avenue. He has his coffee and reads two or three newspapers then heads over to his office. He's usually there between seven and seven thirty."

"Great, thanks. I think I'll have a cup of coffee with Senator big bucks tomorrow. I'll talk to you later."

At five-thirty the next morning, Hamilton Kingsbury punched in the private code to the Senate gym on the first floor of the Russell Senate building. Opened in 1909 after taking five years to build, the Russell building, named for former Senator Richard Russell Jr. of Georgia, is the oldest of the Senate buildings. The building's Beaux-Arts architectural style draws thousands of visitors each year. The high arches and columns are the perfect backdrop for snapshots to send grandma and the rest of the family back home.

The gym is one of the last bastions of the "good-old-boys club." The space is often used for lobbying amongst the senators for their pet projects and other sorts of deal making. Kingsbury started his workout with a 15 minute treadmill warm up followed by 30 minutes on an elliptical machine, then 15 minutes of upper body weightlifting. *It's a great day*, he thought to himself as he worked his arms and legs on the elliptical. He was thinking of some of the decorative changes he'd make to the White House when he was President. He was also thinking of who he could pick for his Chief of Staff. It had to be someone as ruthless as he was, but more importantly, someone totally loyal to him and someone he could totally trust. He finished his workout, showered, dressed and walked outside to his waiting limousine.

Jack was sitting near the window of the Starbucks reading the *Washington Post* when the Senator's limousine drove up. He sipped his coffee and watched as the Senator stepped out of the limo and pulled the collar up on his cashmere topcoat to ward off the morning chill. Kingsbury came in, walked to the front of the line and laid a five dollar bill on the counter without saying a word, then went straight to the pickup area where his drink was waiting for him. It was clear he was well known here. The Senator made his way to the back of the coffee shop and sat at a small table just big enough for a chair on either side with room to spread out a newspaper. Jack picked up his coffee as he rose from his chair and followed Kingsbury's path and sat down opposite the Senator.

"If you're looking for a statement for your paper you need to come by my office and pick up a press release. It has all the current information you'll need for an article."

"I'm not with any newspaper Senator," he said flatly. The Senator looked up.

"Then you're just some stranger interrupting my morning coffee. It's been less than a pleasure talking to you. Now go away."

"Not gonna happen Senator. I have a few questions about the recent meeting at your ranch with a bunch of Middle East oil people."

The Senator again looked up from his newspaper, took a sip of his coffee, gave Jack a menacing stare and said"What goes on at my ranch is none of your business. Now, I am telling you again and for the last time, go away and leave me alone."

Jack saw right away that the wealthy Senator was used to getting his way. He was thinking of what to say next when he felt a heavy hand pressing down heavily on his right shoulder. He looked up and saw what must have been a six-five, three hundred-twenty pound linebacker body guard.

"Is there a problem Senator?" the linebacker drawled as he put his hand on Jack's shoulder. Jack had seen the huge guy sitting alone on the other side of the coffee shop but paid him no mind. He figured the giant was a linebacker for the Redskins. He should have known Kingsbury wouldn't travel without a bodyguard.

"No problem at all," the Senator said, "Mr....?"

"Wilder, Jack Wilder."

"Mr. Wilder was just leaving."

Jack felt the hand turn into a fist full of his jacket and shoulder as the guy stepped back half lifting Jack out of his seat.

"Okay Senator, I'll see you some other time, probably in court after we get the subpoena for all your records and events at your ranch along with your office planning calendar."

"Fat chance of that," the Senator replied. "Do you know who I am?"

"I do, as a matter of fact. You're a Presidential candidate who's about to get his name in the news for obstructing a government investigation."

Jack stood the rest of the way up and shrugged his shoulders a couple of times to get his jacket back in place as the linebacker released his grip. A few heads turned as he casually walked out of the coffee shop leaving the Senator to think about what he'd said. He had no real authority or cause for any kind of subpoena or anything else, but the Senator didn't know that, yet. Although it certainly wouldn't take him long to figure it out.

The Senator stood and threw his newspapers down on the table. His neck was already flushed and his face was quickly catching up. His face was starting to turn red as he stormed out of the coffee shop.

"Get me Ballinger, and get him now, I want him in my office in a half hour!" he fumed to the bodyguard as he stormed outside to his waiting limousine. Jack had known he probably wouldn't get anything out of the Senator. His main intent was merely to rattle him a little. And as he glanced back over his shoulder on his way out, he too could see the bloom coming on and knew he had done just that.

Chapter 40

Kingsbury stormed through the lobby of his office without looking up or acknowledging any of his staff. Each of them looked at the floor as the raging tornado blew by. They knew from past experience when to give the man a wide berth and this was clearly one of those times. Many staffers had made the mistake of trying to appease the Senator when he was in such a state, and all had been summarily dismissed. Their positions didn't matter, senior staff or intern, they were immediately chucked out the door. Kingsbury marched into his office and slammed the door behind him. Paintings on the walls rattled and shook as if they, too, were afraid of the man and his childish temper tantrum.

Kingsbury was still fuming and about to explode an hour and a half later when Ballinger opened the door to his office, came in and closed the door behind him. "What's up?" he asked, as he walked across the room.

"What's up? What's up? I'll tell you what the hell is up, you imbecile! Jack Wilder invited himself to have a cup of coffee with me this morning. Jack Wilder! I thought you said he was taken care of. I thought you said he was staying busy with the Houston police fending off a murder charge. I thought you said he was out of the picture." He let out a disgusted breath and pushed back hard from his opulent desk. "I thought I could count on you to do one simple little thing. Clearly, I am the only one thinking around here. It sure as hell isn't you. You're not as smart as I thought you were. In fact, I think you're nothing more than the village idiot."

"You know Senator, sometime you can be a real pain in the ass," Ballinger said as he casually turned and walked over to an original RC Gorman painting hanging on the wall. "And if you don't get a handle on that temper of yours, one of these days you're gonna blow a vein and have a stroke. You'll end up being an invalid in a nursing home with no one to come and see you, kinda like your dear old mother." Ballinger took a step back, tilted his head a little and surveyed the Gorman. He stepped forward, grasped the two bottom corners of the expensive painting and shifted it slightly back into a level position. "You know, a painting like this would be more suitable to the New Mexico Senator's office than yours, don't ya think?" he said as he turned and walked out the door.

"Get back in here you ungrateful bastard!" A red faced Kingsbury screamed as he slammed his fist down on his desk, every vein in his head bulging like it was going to explode. Ballinger calmly walked on through the suite of offices without looking back.

"Get back here!," Kingsbury shouted again as he picked up a paperweight and cocked his arm back to throw it, looking like a major league pitcher readying for a fast ball. He looked through the open door at all the faces staring back at him. Then, just as quickly, each head immediately looked down again and everyone went back to work. No one said a word.

They had seen it before. They all held their collective breaths, waiting for the storm to blow over.

Kingsbury took a deep breath, put the paperweight down, adjusted his tie and calmly walked across the room to close the door. The bright red slowly faded from his cheeks as his normal color crept back into his face. He realized Ballinger probably wasn't coming back, ever. He walked back to his desk and sat, staring into space, thinking. Ballinger knew too much. If he had indeed quit, he needed to be taken out of service permanently. First things first though, there was a presidential campaign to start. He'd give Ballinger a week or so to come to his senses before ordering anything radical. It really didn't matter whether Ballinger came back or not. Either way Ballinger would be eliminated. He had to be made an example of. People needed to know the consequences of defying Hamilton Kingsbury, III.

Ballinger skipped down the stairs to the second floor and slipped into the men's room. He chose the furthest stall and ducked in. He delicately withdrew the small receiver/recorder from his coat pocket, plugged in the earpiece and listened for a couple of minutes. The bug he'd placed on the Gorman painting was working well. He could hear and record everything in Kingsbury's office, as clearly as if he were a fly on the wall. He was sure he could gain a lot of good information to go along with all the tapes he had copied from the events at the Senator's ranch. He carefully placed the receiver behind the cool porcelain tank of the toilet. He'd be back later to retrieve it.

Ballinger had already made his decision to leave the Senator's employment and the quick tempered maniac made it easy for him to solidify his decision. People with tempers like that always made costly mistakes somewhere along the line. Ballinger had no intention of being around when the Senator made his.

Ballinger did a rough calculation of the dollar amounts he had in his overseas accounts. The total was close to five million, give or take a few bucks, more than enough to disappear and take some time off before going back to work. Before he could leave though, he had one more job to do, one that wouldn't pay anything. He knew the Senator would see him as a loose end that had to be trimmed. He figured he'd have a week at best before Kingsbury sent someone to kill him. That meant he had a week to get everything arranged.

Chapter 41

After leaving the Senator, Jack decided to drive west to CIA headquarters in Langley. He figured his boss would like an update and it was a great day for a drive. The sun was shining with only a few gray clouds in the sky. It was a balmy sixty degrees and traffic was light this time of day, or as light as it could be for Washington. He headed west across the Theodore Roosevelt Memorial bridge, took the ramp onto Washington Memorial Parkway and headed north along the Potomac admiring the sailboats on the river as he drove. The wind was starting to pick up and some of the gray clouds were melting together looking to ruin what had been a gorgeous day only five minutes earlier. Huge white sails billowed as the sleek-hulled boats heeled over in the stiff wind. As Jack drove along, he pictured himself at the helm of one of the sailing wonders with Celeste at his side.

The CIA headquarters' building is made up of five long rectangular buildings, each close to five stories high. The entire grouping totals just over two and a half million square feet. The huge complex sits in the middle of two hundred and fifty-eight acres on the Virginia side of the Potomac River. The cornerstone of the original building was laid by President Dwight Eisenhower in 1959. The actual number of employees working for the CIA, along with the agency's budget, are two of the many classified government mysteries.

Jack showed his credentials to the guard at the gate and parked in the secured employee lot. He showed his credentials again as he entered the door to the main lobby. He took a second to admire the sixteen-foot circle of granite in the middle of the lobby. He'd seen it hundreds of times, but it always served as a reminder for what the CIA stood for, of what *he* stood for. The granite is inlaid with an American Bald Eagle, a shield, and a sixteen point compass. The eagle represents strength, the shield defense and the compass intelligence from around the world. He walked across the huge granite seal and headed upstairs to Alan Blackwell's office.

"Is he in, Moneypenny?" Jack asked the beautiful blonde assistant who sat outside Blackwell's office. She was a knockout whose last name was really Dickinson. Jack couldn't help himself, when he was around her and in the CIA headquarters he was James Bond. Besides, she was much prettier than any of the movie Moneypennys.

"For you, always James," she replied as Jack winked at her and strolled into Blackwell's office.

Blackwell stood, walked around his desk and met Jack halfway across the room. They shook hands and Blackwell motioned to the leather couch on the wall opposite his desk. Jack took a seat on the couch and Blackwell sat across from him in an overstuffed, cordovan leather chair. Moneypenny brought in a tray of coffee and set it on the table between them.

"So Jack," Blackwell said as he poured two cups of coffee, "what have you learned?"

"There is no oil shortage."

"What?"

"No oil shortage. The pieces finally came together. Barry the Wonder Boy actually was the first to see it. Palacios figured it out and was about to tell the world. Somebody killed him to keep it quiet. Still don't know who killed him, but I'm getting closer."

"Hmm," Blackwell said as he grabbed his coffee cup with both hands and sank further back into the leather chair. The warmth of the cup was comforting. He had a feeling the ensuing conversation wouldn't be. "So you're telling me that the whole shortage thing is totally made up?"

"Yup."

"Okay…so… who would have the power to do something like that?"

Jack glanced out the window; the wind had totally shoved the dark clouds together. Rain was on the way again.

"Well, we're still sifting through all the data, but to pull it off it would take some substantial horsepower from several of the heavy duty OPEC countries and, of course, some high powered folks in the U.S. oil industry. One person of interest is none other than Senator Hamilton Kingsbury, III, Chairman of the Committee on Energy and Natural Resources. He recently had a summit meeting at his ranch in Montana and several oil people from the Middle East were in attendance. He somehow managed to keep it out of the papers."

Jack swallowed the last sip of his coffee, reached for the carafe from the table and poured himself another cup. He paused a second to study the steam as it rose from his cup.

"Another interesting thing is that a guy named Bryson Chandler, CEO of Global Oil where Trini Palacios was once employed, was killed in a car wreck not far from the Senator's ranch around the same time all the oil heavyweights were meeting there. The control of Global Oil comes through a variety of shell corporations that all trace back to the Senator himself. If I had to bet on it, my money would be on the Senator. I think he is behind the whole deal."

"You're telling me that a sitting U.S .Senator, one who is running for President no less, could be the master mind of an international conspiracy?"

"Yes I am boss. Proving It, on the other hand, ain't gonna be easy. But the data Wonder Boy came up with sure points in that direction," Jack said as he set his cup on the table and stood to leave.

"Okay," Blackwell said as Jack stepped towards the door. "Keep me posted. And one other thing, when you have some time you might want to fill me in on the dead guy in your girlfriend's apartment and the three drug dealers you came across down in Texas who also managed to get themselves killed."

"Huh," Jack said as he shrugged his shoulders, "Don't have any idea what you're talking about."

Jack stopped by Barry's desk on his way out. "Anything new to report?" he asked.

"Nothing, nada, zero, zippo."

"Okay, I have a quick favor to ask."

"Ask away Spymaster."

"I want you to give this guy a call," he said, as he handed him Detective Bonham's card.

"He's with the Houston PD. As soon as he answers, just say – "Angelina Shepherd killed her husband. The gun is in her closet." Nothing more and nothing less, then hang up. Don't say another word."

"I'm not even gonna ask." The computer whiz replied. "I'll do it right away."

"Thanks kid." Jack hesitated for a second, flipped an errant paperclip on Barry's desk back into the holder, then turned and left.

Jack's cell phone rang just as he reached his car. He turned his back to the car, leaned against the door and answered: "Mr. Wilder… it's Damon Escobares. You asked me to call you if I found out anything else. Well, after you left I did a little snooping on my own. The more I look at it, the more I think there is no oil shortage. Hold on a sec." Jack heard footsteps as the young man walked across his office and closed the door. "Okay, I'm back," Escobares said in a low voice.

"So what have you found out?"

"Well, I was able to get into Trini's computer late last night after everyone had gone home. I was looking for a file or a directory where he might have hidden something and I came across a file called Great American Baseball Players. I thought that was strange because Trini and I once had a conversation about baseball. He told me he hated it and that next to hockey it was probably the most boring sporting event ever invented. He said soccer was really the only sport that anyone cared about."

Jack felt a few drops of rain hit his head. He looked up at the darkening sky, climbed into the driver's seat and closed the door with one hand, holding his cell to his ear with the other. Just as he closed the door, the downpour hit, like water going over a dam.

"Anyway," Escobares continued, "there were a few pages about ball players and their statistics, boring stuff to anyone who would read it. After the boring stuff, I found an outline or rather a timeline that Trini had created with dates and notes about cables, emails and other documents he had uncovered. I printed the entire file, turned off his computer and left."

"Great work Damon, have you told this to anyone else?"

"No, I'm afraid to."

"Good, you should be afraid. This is some pretty serious stuff."

"What should I do?"

Jack thought about it for a few seconds as he stared through the windshield at the pouring rain. He felt like he was in a carwash. "Take down this address," Jack said as he rattled off Barry the Wonder Boy's name and address. "Now, I want you to get to the closest Fed Ex office and overnight it. Don't use any of the mailing facilities at your office. Then I want you to forget all of it and don't do anymore snooping."

"I can do that, Mr. Wilder."

"Damon, I'm serious. You have done too much already, although I really do appreciate it. I want to be sure you don't put yourself in any danger. Do not, do not under any circumstances share any of this information with anyone."

"Okay, I won't."

Jack said goodbye to Damon, started the car and flipped on the windshield wipers. The rain had lessened, but only slightly. He called Wonder Boy's office phone as he drove out of the parking lot and left him a voice mail telling him to expect another package of data to look at. He spent the next two days cleaning his apartment, drinking beer with Angus, paying a few bills and catching up on correspondence. Then it was back to Houston.

Chapter 42

Angelina stepped out of her marble shower, dried off her slender body and artfully knotted herself in the towel. She stood in front of the mirror staring at the condensation. She leaned closer to the mirror, wiped some of it away with the palm of her hand and studied the tiny wrinkles at the edges of her eyes. She hated to admit it, but she was beginning to age, or maybe the wrinkles came from stress. Stress you get from being pressured by the likes of Jack Wilder. She was getting fed up with his constant intrusions into her otherwise perfect life. She had all the best things. There was a nice house, a yellow corvette, memberships in the finest clubs and lots of money from two insurance policies from two deceased husbands. She still had her looks, looks that turned heads. She worked hard at keeping her body in shape. The only thing missing was peace of mind, the kind she couldn't get with Wilder constantly harassing her.

She finished her hair and makeup, wandered into the huge walk-in closet, opened her lingerie drawer and picked out a red thong. She held it suspended delicately…then decided against that approach. She decided to go commando. It was going to be that kind of night on the town. She needed some fun and some tension release. If the right opportunity came up, she didn't want some handsome stranger getting tangled up in her underwear. She put on a short black, sleeveless, chiffon cocktail dress.

As she scanned the rest of her closet her eyes came to rest on the box of Jimmy Choo platforms. She knew there weren't shoes in the box. She raised her eyebrows as she eyed the box. *Hmm*.... She pulled the box off the shelf, took the top off and stared at the gun inside. "Come to mama," she said as she lifted the weapon from its hiding place and pointed it at herself in the full length mirror next to the shelves of shoes. "So long, Wilder," she said as she mimed shooting the gun. She held the pistol with the top of the barrel pointed up and level with her lips and blew across the top of it like Fatima Blush had done in one of the Bond movies. She knew how to load the gun. She knew how to shoot the gun. At first she had thought about getting rid of it, but now was glad she'd kept it.

The gun felt a little heavy and cumbersome in her hands when she killed Garrison, but it had worked out well in the end. The hardest part had been getting his body in the trunk of the rented Mercedes then getting it out again when she dumped it out by the airport. All those upper body exercises at the gym had paid off. As far as she knew she was in the clear. The cops really had nothing to go on and hadn't come around to talk to her anymore. If it worked once, it could work again. With a little luck, this time she wouldn't even have to put a body in a trunk. She would lure Jack somewhere isolated and kill him. Too bad she thought, he's kind of handsome. She put the gun back in the box, replaced the lid and set the box back on the shelf between the $1,400 Gucci pumps and the $2,000 Manolo Blahnik stilettos. She felt a tad bit of the stress fade away as she finished dressing, picked out a gold Gucci purse and headed down the stairs.

As she reached the bottom of the stairs the doorbell chimed. She opened the door and saw a familiar face that she couldn't quite place. He was wearing a wrinkled dark blue pinstriped suit with a white shirt and pale yellow tie. The tie had what looked like the slightest hint of a ketchup stain near the tip.

"Mrs. Shepherd…. Detective Bonham from the Houston Police Department. I spoke to you shortly after your husband was killed. I'm not sure you remember me…." Her eyes opened wide as the panic set in.

"Of course I do," she replied struggling to keep her calm demeanor. "What can I do for you detective? Whatever it is, I hope it won't take up much time. As you can see, I'm just on my way out for the evening."

Bonham looked around a bit and took a step closer to the door. "Well, here's the thing. We got this strange call from someone who didn't identify himself. He said you were the one who had killed your husband and that the gun was in your house." Bonham intentionally didn't say closet. If the tip was true he didn't want to spook the woman into tossing the gun. "I know it sounds pretty crazy, but I was wondering if I could come in and have a quick look around."

"Well… well… that's just... uh… just, but pure nonsense," Angelina said, still trying to keep her composure. She fidgeted a bit with the red silk scarf at her neck. She could feel the palms of her hands beginning to sweat. "As I said, I was just on my way out. I really don't have time for you to start snooping around."

"It will only take a minute or two," the detective persisted. He took a half step toward her. He could smell her perfume reaching out to him.

"I'm sorry, I just can't, I just can't let you in," she said. "If you're accusing me of something, shouldn't you have one of those warrant things or something, and shouldn't I have a lawyer?"

"No accusations ma'am, just trying to do my job. I'm sure the caller was just some kind of whacko. I just wanted to look around so I can put a note in the file saying it's unfounded. If I didn't at least make an attempt, I wouldn't be doing my job now, would I?"

"Well, I'm just going to have to think about it detective. If part of your job is coming up with lame excuses to get into people's homes then you're really not very smart and probably in the wrong line of work. Maybe you should consider some kind of door to door sales, like vacuum cleaners. Now, if you will excuse me, I really am on my way out," she stepped back from him abruptly, closed the door and left him standing there face to face with the peep hole.

Angelina turned and leaned against the door, breathing heavily. Her heart was pumping so hard it felt like it was going to come out of her chest. She held her breath and listened, hoping to hear Bonham's footsteps as he left. As he walked away Bonham was thinking, *you're right lady, I need a warrant and it would be a cold day in hell before a judge would give me one just because some whacko called and said you had a gun in your closet. Still, there must be something there, or you wouldn't have been in such a hurry to get rid of me.*

It seemed like an eternity, but she finally heard him fumble with his keys, start his car and drive away. It slowly came to her as she pushed herself away from the door. *Wilder! He had to have been in her house. Who else could it have been?* She took a deep breath and a mountain of rage burst into her mind. "Wilder, you son-of-a-bitch," she screamed as she threw her $2,400 Gucci handbag across the foyer, hitting a vase of flowers. The beautiful arrangement of roses, baby's breath and carnations met an untimely end as the expensive vase crashed onto the marble floor. She stomped past the broken glass on her way to the kitchen where she grabbed a $90 bottle of Merlot and a glass out of the wine cabinet. She plopped down on the cold kitchen floor, poured some wine and began to think of what to do, how to get rid of Jack. A night on the town and what could have been a great one night stand had quickly been replaced by her renewed hatred for Wilder.

This was the last straw. If she was ever going to get on with her life she could only do it with Jack Wilder out of the picture. Completely. Totally. And forever. Forever, as in no-longer- among-the-living. She took a long sip of the Merlot and stared at the opposite wall with laser like intensity. Upstairs, looking into the mirror and holding the gun had been a kind of game, a kind of fantasy. Now it needed to become a reality. She finished the glass of Merlot. "Wilder," she said, as she filled her glass with the last few drops in the bottle, "you done messed with the wrong woman."

Chapter 43

Two days later Ballinger drove his Porsche to the Washington Highlands neighborhood in Southeast DC. The neighborhood was number 22 on the FBI's top 25 list of most dangerous neighborhoods in the United States. He parked on the corner of Atlantic Avenue and Fourth Street. He hated to get rid of the sports car, but if he was going to disappear he couldn't very well do it driving around in a 2010 Porsche Carrera. The car was red with black trim and beige Corinthian leather seats. The explosive set of wheels could do zero to sixty in 5.4 seconds with a top speed of 150 mph.

He'd paid just over $80,000 cash for it and registered it in the name of Elmer Fudd. The clerk at the Motor Vehicle Department didn't even raise an eyebrow or ask for his identification when he gave her the name. All he did was slip the paperwork across the counter with a hundred dollar bill attached to the back with a paperclip.

He left the key in the ignition and called a cab. He figured in that neighborhood, the car would be a joy ride for someone in less than an hour. With a little luck, some punk could drive it for a day or so before attracting the attention of the cops.

The cabbie dropped him off at the Hart Senate Office Building. He took the stairs two at a time up to the second floor, retrieved the receiver from the men's room, and slipped it into his coat pocket. He thought about calling a cab again as he left the building but decided to walk instead. He was wearing running shoes, jeans, a tan Robert Old cashmere sweater over a pastel yellow Ralph Lauren dress shirt and a black Moncler down jacket. The sun was shining and the weather was a chilly 41 degrees, a great day for a brisk walk.

Ballinger walked to the closest coffee shop, one of the few in the area that wasn't a Starbucks, and ordered a tall, black, house coffee. He took his preferred seat next to the window toward the back of the shop. There were only two other customers in the small establishment. Ballinger looked down the block at the Starbucks, nearly full. *Market dynamics,* he thought, *the little guy doesn't have much of a chance anymore.*

He plugged the earpiece into the receiver and pressed play. Just as he had suspected, the first thing the Senator did was tell one of his minions to find a replacement for him who wouldn't cause problems. Ballinger heard Kingsbury's office door close, then about half of the Senator's phone call to Bastrop.

Bastrop was the phony name of a go-to middle man in Brussels with a dozen answering services retrieving calls under a dozen different company names. He was the guy rich and powerful people called when they wanted someone eliminated. Philandering spouses, political enemies, business enemies, it made no difference to Bastrop. If you wanted them gone and had the money to pay, he was your guy. Bastrop always spoke through a voice modulator to eliminate the possibility of voice recognition. He sounded like Darth Vader when he talked on the phone. Any direct connection to him was totally untraceable.

It was Bastrop who had connected Ballinger with the Senator for the Vienna hit. After that, the Senator had dealt directly with the former Marine. The biggest mistake the Senator had made was talking directly to Ballinger with the details about Palacios after Bastrop had connected the two of them. That particular conversation was the first recording Ballinger had made of the Senator.

Ballinger heard the Senator say there was no urgency, but he needed someone to do a job for him in the U.S. in a week or so. Ballinger breathed a small sigh of relief as he took a sip of his hot coffee. He knew he had an extra day or so to complete his plans and disappear. The Senator was cunning and ruthless when it came to getting his way, but he was clueless when it came to making sure his people were covering all the bases that could lead back to him. He had always assumed that no one would ever have the guts to cross him.

Ballinger finished his coffee and caught a cab back to his apartment in Hyattsville, Maryland. The apartment was in a newer complex with all the amenities, a pool, fitness center and clubhouse. The only one he ever used was the fitness center and always late at night when few were people around.

The apartment itself was a modern, one bedroom unit on the third floor with a kitchen full of the latest stainless steel appliances. The place was small, but well suited for his needs. He never spoke to any of the neighbors and always kept a low profile. It was the same with the other three apartments he currently rented; one in France, one in Brazil and one in Australia. He always paid for six months rent in advance and all were leased under different names. No one ever questioned him. Each place came furnished and could be left in an instant without a trace of who the occupant had been.

He slipped off his jacket, slung it over the bar stool at the kitchen counter and walked down the short hall to the bedroom. He stepped into the closet and pulled an old medium sized cardboard box off the shelf. He carried the box to the bed and opened the flaps. The top of the box held a few towels and wash cloths. He set those aside and emptied the rest of the contents, all DVD's onto the bed. He studied the jewel cased sleeves on a few of them for a minute or so. He scooped them up and carried them back into the kitchen where he methodically placed them face up on the table.

Each one had been carefully labeled with times, dates and names of the principal players. He brought the DVD player provided with the furnished apartment into the kitchen from the bedroom, made himself a pot of coffee, and sat down and spent the next several hours watching, listening and making notes. Afterwards he pulled on a pair of latex gloves and carefully cleaned each disk and case. He referred back to his notes, pulled out the critical ones he was going to use and shredded the rest, along with his notes. He emptied the shredder into a trash bag, sealed it with a twist tie and dropped it down the trash chute in the hallway. Then he returned to his apartment and packaged up the remaining DVD's by wedging them into a medium-sized express mail box while the Post Office TV sales pitch, "If it fits, it ships," popped into his head.

Early the next morning he walked to the post office just around the block and filled out a mailing label with Celeste's Houston address. He smiled to himself as he inked "Hart Senate Building" as the return address. He handed the package to the surly clerk behind the counter. She had a blonde dye job that had gone bad weeks ago. Brown and gray roots were fighting their way to the surface. Her scratched, crooked wire rim glasses sat on an oversized nose attached to a face with a built in, permanent scowl. Her official U.S. Post Office shirt had several coffee stains on it and looked like it hadn't been near a washing machine since Nixon was President. Ballinger figured her for the type who would see how far she could throw a package marked fragile before putting it in the correct bin. He smiled at the cranky clerk just to see if her facial expression would change. It didn't. He paid cash for the postage and left.

Ballinger's first thought had been to kill the Senator, but overall this was a much better plan. The Senator would be arrested, deny everything of course, and spend the next year working with a battalion of lawyers paying them enormous sums of money to keep him out of prison, which probably wouldn't work. And if the Senator didn't end up in prison, Ballinger could always come back later and kill the guy himself. He figured Kingsbury would be way too busy trying to stay out of the slammer than to come after him. As a little extra insurance, Ballinger made a deal with Bastrop: If the Senator called for a hit on Ballinger, Ballinger would double the fee and reverse the target back to the Senator. He knew Bastrop had no allegiances when it came to making money and he'd be more than happy to take the deal. As he hung up the phone, Bastrop hoped the Senator would call; it would be by far the most profitable deal he had ever made.

After returning from the post office, Ballinger gathered up his travel bag which included $20,000 in cash, as well as a couple of bogus passports and credit cards. He set the bag by the front door and called a cab and then he wiped down every surface in the apartment with handi wipes while he waited for his ride. It didn't take long. He stuffed the used wipes in his pocket; they would go in a trash can at the airport. He closed the door to the apartment and walked outside into the cool Maryland air just as the cab pulled up. "Reagan National," he said to the cabbie as he opened his phone. The weather app said it was sunny and fifty degrees outside his apartment on Av de Messine in Paris.

Chapter 44

Two days later, Celeste was awakened by a knock on her door. She slipped on a robe, glanced over at a sleeping Jack and went to the door. A cheery postman with a bright smile said "Good morning," as he handed her the package from the Hart building. She dropped the package on the kitchen table and went back to the bedroom for a few more minutes of snuggling with Jack. He came to life as she crawled in beside him. He turned toward her and used his knee to lift the bottom edge her nightgown. "Hmm, morning sex, what a great way to start the day," she said, as she rolled over on top of him and kissed him behind the ear.

A half hour later they both stepped into the steamy shower and took turns washing each other's backs.

"What do you have planned for today," Jack asked.

"Not much, thought I'd spend an hour or so at the shooting range. I'm really starting to get into this shooting thing. What about you?"

"I'm gonna hang out here this afternoon and review all the stuff and ideas I have accumulated to try and figure out my next step. I think this whole thing is about to break wide open."

"That's great," she said as she stepped out of the shower and wrapped a huge towel around her body and a smaller one around her wet head. Why don't we walk down to Starbucks for a bit to get some coffee and something to eat? After that we'll come back here and you can pretend you're Sherlock Holmes and solve this whole thing."

"I like that idea," he said as he tied a towel around his waist, kissed her on the back of the neck and poked a toothbrush into his mouth.

It was a pleasant day for a walk. Not a lot of humidity, rare for Houston this time of year. The sun was shining and the air was clear. A few clouds floated around like giant cotton balls against a pale blue sky. After they had walked a couple of blocks, Celeste reached over and took Jack's hand. He thought they looked like a couple of high school kids on their way to class or maybe headed out on a date.

"If we were in school," she said, as if she had read his mind "would you offer to carry my books?"

"I don't know, aren't women supposed to be liberated these days? I'd think they would want to carry their own books."

"Hmm," she said, as he smiled and opened the door to a very crowded Starbucks. He held the door, waiting for her to go inside.

The Starbucks was one of the newer ones with lots of granite countertops and brand new shelving displaying the latest in Starbucks cups, brewing machines and other coffee-related items. Four small, comfortable looking leather chairs sat around an antique looking coffee table off to one side of the room. All four were occupied by people reading newspapers. Every other table in the place was occupied. Morning people trying to get caffeine jump starts to the busy day ahead. A young couple at a table near the window got up and left. Jack snagged their table while Celeste went to order. She returned with a tall vanilla latte for herself, a large black coffee for Jack, and two ham and egg breakfast sandwiches.

"Oh, I almost forgot," she said as she sat everything down on the table. "That knock at the door that got me out of bed this morning was the postman delivering a package for you. Were you expecting something?"

"Not that I know of," he said as he took a large bite out of his breakfast sandwich. They talked about the merits of the Glock vs. the Walther as well as her job, his job, and a variety of other things while they finished up their breakfast. On the walk back Jack once again made a display out of opening the door for Celeste as they left. This time it was he who took her hand as she came through the door.

When they returned to the apartment they found the generously proportioned Detective Glen Rose leaning against the wall next to the front door. He was wearing one of those bright red Hawaiian shirts with big yellow flowers, tan Dockers and black lace up shoes with white socks.

"So what have you two love birds been up to since we last talked?" Rose asked.

"Oh, you know the usual. knocked over a couple of 7-11's, robbed a bank or two, printed a few million in counterfeit bills, then hung out at Jimmy Hoffa's grave for a bit," Jack quipped. "So what can we do for you detective?"

"Well, here's the thing, Jackie boy. Mr. Duct tape in your apartment turned out to be one Carmine Milano. Word has it, he was a hit man from Chicago, a freelance guy who's good at skating on murder charges. We ran ballistics on the nine mil we found in your apartment." Rose hitched his huge frame away from the door and shifted his weight to his other foot. "Turns out, that gun was a match for the slugs we pulled out of Cisco Lopeno and his pals. And here's another thing, the slug we found in Mr. Milano came from the same gun." Rose shifted his weight again. "And, there was no gunshot residue on you, or Ms. Windom, but then I guess you knew that." Rose took a deep breath, made a fist and belched as he pressed the fist against his chest and made a sour face. He reached into his pocket, took out a roll of antacids and popped one into his mouth. "So I'm thinking you may have been telling the truth about someone else being in the apartment. Of course, none of that explains what the late Mr. Milano was doing taped to a chair."

"Can't help you with that," Jack said. "It's like I told you, I came home, there this guy was, taped to a chair, and the next thing I know I'm waking up on the floor with a bad headache." Jack shrugged his shoulders and lifted his arms slightly turning his palms outward to emphasize his point.

"Sure Jack, and I'm thinking that's about as real as the tooth fairy. Either way, looks like the two of you are in the clear for Mr. Milano's demise, but you're both still shining bright on my radar." Rose walked past them then turned back around. "And another thing," he said, "you've got lipstick on your collar."

"Nice socks, Detective," Jack replied, as the huge Hawaiian fashion statement waddled away.

Neither one of them had paid any attention to the small figure wearing a black hoodie walking across the parking lot behind Jack and Celeste. The bill of a dark blue baseball cap barely visible underneath the hood. Unseen eyes stayed hidden behind a pair of dark Prada aviator sunglasses. Black running pants and shoes completed the concealing outfit. The lone figure stopped by a car and bent over under the guise of tying a shoe, all the time carefully studying Wilder.

The love birds went inside. Jack sat down at the kitchen table and used his pocketknife to open the package Celeste had told him about. He began to sort through the contents. It was all DVD's. Celeste went into the bedroom, and changed out of her slacks and sweater into jeans and a sweatshirt, her favorite things to wear to the shooting range. The loose fitting shirt gave her freedom of movement. She opened her dresser drawer and took the Glock 26 out of its holster. She slipped a full magazine into the gun, jacked a round into the chamber, put the safety on and tucked the gun in her purse. It was a habit she had gotten into. She decided early on, if she was carrying a weapon, she would always be ready to use it. She had asked the guy at the shooting range if it was a good idea. "Damn straight," he'd said. "That's the way we do things in Texas."

Jack picked up the box and looked at the return address. "Hmm," he said to himself "who in the Hart Senate building would send me a bunch of DVDs?"

"What?" she said as she came out of the bedroom and headed for the door with a firm hand holding her purse against her hip.

"Oh nothing, just mumbling to myself about the stuff in this box."

"Okay, have fun, Sherlock," she said as she gave him a peck on the cheek and headed for the door.

Chapter 45

Jack carried the DVD's into the living room, popped the first one into the player and hit the play button on the remote. The first thing he saw was gray and white snow then the picture appeared. Standing front and center was none other than Texas Senator and Presidential candidate Hamilton Kingsbury, III. Jack turned up the volume just as the picture widened. He figured the video must have been shot from a ceiling mounted camera. Everything appeared at a downward angle. At first he figured is must have been the Senator giving some kind of political speech to potential donors. Then he noticed an Arab looking gentleman in the audience dressed in a typical Arab Thawb and Keffiyeh. *Odd*, he thought, but then someone like Kingsbury would take money from anywhere he could get it.

He turned the volume up and leaned in closer to the screen. That was when he heard Kingsbury say, "I'm sure you all heard about the tragic death of the OPEC analyst in Vienna. What happened to the gentleman was unfortunate, but it couldn't be helped. We have a great plan in place and it must not be compromised. That fool was about to ruin everything we've worked for." Now the Arab began to speak. "And what of this man, Jack Wilder? What are you doing about him? I understand he has been to Vienna asking lots of questions."

"Whoa," Jack said out loud as he turned the volume up and leaned back in the chair. He heard

Kingsbury respond, "We're dealing with Wilder. We had him followed in Vienna. He spotted our man and accosted him in an alley. Fortunately he bought the story that our guy was from Interpol and had been told to follow him."

Jack couldn't believe what he was seeing and hearing. Who the hell had sent this? He hit the pause button, stood up, ran his fingers through his hair and paced back and forth for a few seconds before sitting back down and hitting the play button again. Kingsbury's voice came back on, "Wilder met with a young OPEC analyst in Vienna named Damon Escobares. Our man assured us that Escobares had nothing concrete to offer Wilder. We will continue to monitor Mr. Wilder and deal with him accordingly if the need arises."

"Be that as it may," Jack heard the Arab respond, "he should never have made the trip to Vienna in the first place. There is too much at stake. He should have already been eliminated. Rest assured, Senator, if you are unable to handle Wilder we will not hesitate to take matters into our own hands. And believe me, that's the last thing you want us to do."

Jack had seen this type before. Lots of tough talk by someone who never got their hands dirty. These kind of guys never did anything themselves. They were dripping with money and quick to spend it to get things done. Then Jack heard Kingsbury say, "I understand, Mr. Iraan. And as I said, we will continue to monitor the situation with Mr. Wilder and deal with it accordingly."

Jack hit the pause button again, grabbed his cell phone and hit the speed dial button for Barry the Wonder Boy.

"Barry, Wilder here," Jack said. I need you to find out everything you can on an Arab named Iraan, and I need it an hour ago."

"Oh, that should be easy enough," Barry said sarcastically. "I'm sure there are only about a million Arabs with that name."

"I'm pretty sure this one has something to do with oil export or production and he's probably pretty high up on the food chain."

"Okay then, that should make it a lot easier. I'll get back to you in a few."

"Thanks, kid," Jack said as he hit the end button on his phone and turned back to the TV.

Jack ejected the first DVD and popped another one in. This one was dated a couple of months earlier and had no video content. It was an audio recording of a conversation between Kingsbury and someone else. "Are you sure you can do it?" he heard the Senator ask.

"It's an easy shot. I've made it hundreds of times anywhere from five hundred to well over three thousand yards," came the reply.

"Just make sure you don't miss. This Palacios guy could mean the end of everything if he blabs to the press. Call me as soon as it's over. If you're successful, the balance of the money will be wired into your account as agreed."

This guy's good, Jack thought to himself. *The Senator had no idea he was being recorded. These kind of guys always give themselves an insurance policy and it looks like this guy is about to cash his in.*

Jack's cell phone rang. It was Barry. "Ok spymaster, here's the scoop. Iraan is way high on the food chain, just like you thought. Turns out he is the one with total control over what gets produced and when. He coordinates with the Arab OPEC representative and directs production to either increase or decrease based on agreements made at the OPEC meetings."

"So, he would have the power to either change production or manipulate the numbers?

"Absolutely."

"Thanks Barry, go out and buy yourself one of those high octane caffeine jolts you like so much."

Jack called Allen Blackwell and filled him in on everything.

"Holy crap, Blackwell groaned, "a sitting U.S. Senator behind all this? That's hard to believe."

"Believe it boss, Kingsbury's a total dirt bag of the highest degree. He has all the money in the world and wants all the power in the world to go with it."

"Ok, send everything to Barry FedEx, highest priority overnight. No, cancel that. On second thought, drive it out to Ellington. I'll call the base commander and have him get one of the jet jockeys from the 147th to fly it straight to Langley Field. That way I'll have it in a few hours and it will be secure. The quicker we get on this thing the better."

"Not a problem," Jack said. "I can get it out to Ellington in a couple of hours."

"Good, I'll start getting everything lined up. Great work Jack."

"Just doing my job boss, you know, keeping the country safe and all that."

Celeste came through the door with her purse slung over her shoulder and a bag of groceries in each arm. Jack was pulling the last DVD out of the player when she came in. She could see his smile and sensed his elation as she headed for the kitchen.

"You look like a kid that just got a new bicycle for Christmas. What's up?" she asked.

"This is it, the key to the whole thing, the ultimate solution."

"What are you talking about?"

"I'm talking about the oil shortage, Trini Palacios' death and the soon to be jail bird Senator Hamilton Kingsbury III. I'm telling ya, the guy's headed for the big house, up the river, the slammer, the joint, the rock, the hoosegow, the house of many doors, stripe city, the gray bar hotel. It's what was in the package that came this morning - DVD recordings, details about everything, people, places, dates and times. It all proves the oil shortage is a scam and gives someone the motive to kill Palacios and it's all on the videos. I'm sure these people had no idea they were being recorded. Whoever did it was inside, someone close to Kingsbury. And now it looks like he's trying to hang his old boss."

Celeste set the groceries on the kitchen counter and gave Jack a hug."Good work, Sherlock," she said.

"Not Sherlock….Bond, *James Bond*."

Jack had a wry smile on his face as he gathered everything up and headed for the door. "I've got to get all this stuff out to Ellington. They're going to fly it down to Langley tonight. I'll be back late, don't wait up."

"OK, just be careful," she said. Jack gave her a huge, extra long kiss and headed out the door.

Chapter 46

Blackwell stayed very busy late into the night informing the higher ups at the CIA, calling the U.S. Attorney General, the DSS, and the FBI. Everyone sat in a conference room drinking coffee and soft drinks late into the night, arguing about which agency had jurisdiction over the case. The DSS argued they had jurisdiction because they were the Federal Law Enforcement Arm of the Department of State with jurisdiction both inside and outside the United States. It was obvious other countries were involved. The FBI, of course, argued that their jurisdiction covered violations in over two hundred categories of federal crime. Clearly this crime would fall into one of those two hundred categories.

In the end, in typical government fashion, they all agreed to disagree and hold off until they could review all the information on an F4 fighter jet headed their way. The decision was made to meet again at six the next morning.

It was a Thursday, and all the players arrived to fresh coffee and pastries at five forty-five that morning. All were eager to be part of the team that would bring down a U.S. Senator. Each one was thinking of the huge political capital they would gain when their agency pulled it off. They all sat around a long, oval, conference table in a secure conference room on the second floor of CIA headquarters. Their expensive leather briefcases stuffed with legal briefs and opinions sat open and at the ready. Somehow overnight a barrage of lawyers from the White House, the FBI and the DSS had gotten themselves into the mix. Blackwell called the meeting to order, a technician pushed a button and the lights in the room dimmed. Then the first video came up showing the exchange between Kingsbury and the Arab. A hush fell over the room as the video played. No one took a sip of coffee or a bite of pastry.

Every conceivable possibility of consequence and fallout was considered and discussed at length. What would the American people think? What effect would it have on the President? What effect would it have on the economy? Who else on the Senator's staff might be involved? Should other governments of the other countries be informed? In the end it was decided that the U.S. would air its dirty laundry at home rather than on an international stage. The US Attorney General indicated that the President's preference was for the FBI to handle the case. The President strongly felt, the AG said, that the only way not to make a spectacle of it internationally was to have it handled by the folks over at the Hoover Building. Subtle phone calls would be made afterwards to the Royal Family in Saudi Arabia and heads of state in the other OPEC countries involved. Each country would be left to its own devices as to how they would handle their situation. Of course, the President's option won the day.

All the plans had been put into place. Later that day one of the many satellite eyes in the sky was routed over the Senator's Montana ranch compliments of the CIA. Images were immediately broadcast to the FBI equivalent of the White House "war room."

At six o'clock the following morning, the two gate guards at the Senator's compound in Northern Montana raised their AK-47's and pointed them at the Montana State Police S.W.A.Tvehicle as it sped towards the compound. It was followed by four black Suburbans and two Montana State Police cars. The S.W.A.T vehicle screeched to a stop as 10 heavily armed officers climbed out and pointed their own AK's at the startled guards who immediately lowered their weapons. The guards were armed and loyal but they weren't stupid. An FBI agent jumped out of the lead vehicle, came forward and showed them the search warrant. The State Police officers handcuffed the guards and locked them in the back seats of their patrol cars. They were pretty sure pointing an AK-47 at a Federal Agent was bound to be breaking some kind of law.

The Feds thanked the S.W.A.T guys and sent them on their way with the gate guards in tow. The rest of the group swooped into the compound and grabbed every cell phone, video camera, monitor and computer in the place. Every drawer and cabinet door was opened and every bed was turned over. Everyone was hard at work looking for any clue or detail that could be used to go after the corrupt Senator. At exactly the same time the same thing was happening at the Senator's office and home, only without the firepower. Bewildered secretaries, clerks and interns were ushered out of offices and into a nearby conference room where they would all be interrogated at length later in the day.

Kingsbury was arrested and read his rights as he walked out of the Senate gym. He was immediately transported across town to FBI headquarters. "Do you know who I am? Do you know *who* I am?" the Senator shouted as he was being led away in handcuffs. "You fools don't know who you're dealing with. This time next week you will all be standing in the unemployment line."

Jack sat at the end of the opulent FBI conference room, patiently sipping good coffee and waiting for the Senator's arrival. How was it the FBI managed to get better coffee than the CIA? He thought back to his meeting with Evant in Vienna and the room they had been in. Too bad this room was so nice. He would have preferred something more plain, drab, and cold for his chat with the great Hamilton Kingsbury III.

The Senator was brought in and the cuffs removed. His face was beet red, veins bulging from his neck as he sat in a chair adjacent to Jack. He slammed his fist down on the highly polished mahogany conference table. The whole room seemed to shake. Jack took a sip of coffee and turned his face toward the Senator.

"Just what in the hell is going on here?" Kingsbury shouted. Wilder smiled, blew on his hot coffee and took another sip.

"Care for a cup of coffee, Senator?" he asked calmly.

"I'll tell you what you can do with your coffee you no good son-of-a .....Wait a minute, I know you. You're that rude little man from the coffee shop."

"That would be *Mr. Rude Little Man* to you Senator. I'm the rude little man who is about to send you away for a long, long time. Jack took another sip of his coffee, smiled and pushed "play" on a remote control sitting next to his coffee. The huge screen embedded in the far wall burst into light and sound. The scene in the conference room at the ranch was playing.

"Where did you get that?" Kingsbury demanded. "It's a total fabrication; any first year film student could have put that together."

"Actually, they couldn't Senator. And, it's been verified as being quite real by the lab downstairs. These FBI boys really know what they're doing when it comes to that kind of stuff."

"I don't know who you think you are or who you work for pal, but I can tell you this, in another week you'll be out looking for a new job."

"You know, Kingsbury; *you're* the little man here. Your greed and hunger for power is what got you into this mess. And all the lawyers in the world aren't going to be able to get you out of it."

"If you know what's good for you, you will address me as Senator Kingsbury and give me the respect that comes with being a U.S .Senator." Kingsbury's face, which had regained some of its color, began to turn red again. Jack produced the biggest smile he could, knowing that as Kingsbury got more and more angry a slip was bound to happen .

"So let me ask you this, Ham, old buddy, just why was it that you had Trini Palacios killed?"

"Palacios was a nobody! He was a pencil pushing nosey little fool who was in the way, he…" Suddenly the politician realized he was losing it. "I want my lawyer" he said. With that Jack picked up his coffee, smiled and headed for the door.

"See you in court, Slick," he said as he walked out the door. "He's all yours," he said to the lead FBI agent.

"Great," the agent responded. "We got every word of it on tape."

Chapter 47

Angelina arrived home, changed out of her black velour hoodie outfit and jumped into the shower. She stood there thinking about Jack Wilder and the success of her surveillance of Celeste's apartment complex. She'd gotten a pretty good feel for the lay of the land and was confident that neither Jack nor anyone else in the area had noticed her in the process. She was just another jogger out for a run in the afternoon Houston sunshine. She dried off, put on a robe, and headed downstairs for a drink.

She had timed the drive from her house to Celeste's apartment down to the second. She really didn't know why. She just figured that's what you did when planning something like a robbery or a murder. She'd watched enough television to know that the bad guys only get away with it if they plan everything down to the last detail. She was definitely working out the details. She had called Carmine Milano several times in the last couple of days but always got his voice mail. It was clear that he didn't want, or no longer needed, her business. *Just as well* she thought *save the money and know for sure that no one will ever do any talking.* She went to the kitchen and poured herself a glass of wine.

What she needed was an iron-clad alibi, something that would put her somewhere else when she was actually pulling the trigger. How could she be in two places at once? She would prefer to be clear across the country or at least one or two states away.

Then it came to her as she was taking her first sip of the wine. She would need to pick a busy travel day, one of those days when airlines overbook and ask people to give up their seats. It was a frequent occurrence at Southwest Airlines. She could buy a ticket then not go. She thought about it then said to herself "No, wouldn't work. They scan the tickets as you board and would know I never got on the damn plane." *Hmm*...she took another sip and gently chewed her lower lip. She scrunched up her nose, raised her eyebrows and said aloud, "That's it, they scan the ticket, they don't scan you." Another drink of wine, it was all coming together.

Angelina decided she needed to do a practice run. Early the next morning she booked herself on a 5:00 p.m. flight from Hobby Field in Houston to Los Angeles. She wore the most common thing she could think of to the airport; inexpensive black slacks, a pale yellow blouse and a light gray sweater. She put just a touch of color on her face and arrived at the airport about thirty minutes before her flight. Her boarding pass number was B10. She lined up with the other B passengers when their boarding group was called. She studied each of them carefully and found one whose boarding pass was sitting loosely in her purse. She carefully lifted it out of the woman's purse and dropped her own pass on the floor. Then she tapped the woman on the shoulder and said "I believe your boarding pass fell out of your purse." The woman looked at her purse, thanked Angelina and picked up the boarding pass. Bingo, mission accomplished.

Angelina pushed herself between a couple of fellow passengers, "Excuse me," she said sweetly and walked across the busy corridor to another gate where she took a seat. She casually watched the woman with whom she had switched boarding passes. Sure enough, the woman handed the ticket agent her pass, the agent scanned it and the new Angelina boarded the flight to Los Angeles. She went home and promptly poured herself another glass of wine. *This could work.*

She looked at the calendar, It was Thursday, April 13th. She made up her mind to do it on Saturday, April 15th. "You know the old saying;" she said to no one, "Nothing is sure except death and taxes." What better day to kill Jack than tax day.

She picked up the phone and made a reservation for the Southwest Airlines7:00 a.m. flight from Houston's Hobby field to Denver on Saturday. Then she called United Airlines and booked a 5:00 p.m. flight from Houston's George Bush Intercontinental airport to Denver. She would take the United flight herself and check into a hotel in Denver. If the police ever asked she would be able to show them the receipt for the Southwest ticket to Denver and the receipt from the Denver hotel where she stayed. She would explain that she went to Denver to do some shopping on the seven am flight and didn't check into her hotel until later because she was shopping and visiting museums. A perfect plan.

Early on the morning of the 15th, Angelina went to the airport to put the first part of her plan in action. She switched boarding passes with a little old lady who was pushing a walker. It was an easy switch and the old gal never had a clue. Angelina left the airport and drove home to put part two of the plan into action.

She thought about calling Carmine one last time. She was confident she could pull it off, but then again, Carmine was a professional who did this sort of thing for a living. Still no answer. After six rings, she gave up. She was on her own now, had to do it herself. She opened the freezer and took the nine mil out of the middle of the bag of frozen peas. After her visit from Bonham, she'd decided a better hiding place than a shoe box was needed. She turned the oven to 250 and baked the weapon and the empty magazine for three minutes to thaw them out. She took five cartridges from her purse, popped them into the freshly thawed magazine and loaded the weapon.

She stared at herself in the mirror. An old movie with Robert De Niro and Jodi Foster came to mind. The film clip played in her mind. She could see De Niro talking to the mirror "You talking to *me*?" She stared a little longer, then said, "Wilder, this is for you," then "Jack" pause, "this is for you." She tried several versions then changed into the black hoodie outfit and left for Celeste's apartment.

Chapter 48

It was just after 9 a.m. when Angelina arrived at the apartment complex. She drove slowly around the parking lot and found a spot with a clear view of the front door to Celeste's apartment. She backed in and fixed her eyes on the apartment wondering how long it would be until Jack made an appearance. She carefully adjusted her expensive Prada sunglasses and stuck her hands in the front pocket of the velour hoodie. The gun safely tucked inside gave her confidence. She gently stroked the barrel of the weapon like she was petting a cat. Each careful movement of her long slender fingers on the weapon brought her that much closer to her prey.

Jack and Celeste had slept a little later than usual. It was Saturday and neither of them had anything pressing to do.

"It's a great day," Jack said as he sat up in bed and stretched his arms toward the ceiling. "Kingsbury is in the slammer; his battalion of lawyers have spent the last three days trying to get a judge to approve bail. Now everyone has gone home for the weekend which means at least another two days he'll be cooling his heels in a jail cell. And, another minor miracle, as soon as Kingsbury was arrested, the OPEC oil wells that had allegedly gone dry mysteriously came back to life. All the countries involved said they had been shut down for maintenance, not because they had run out of oil. Life is good."

"So, what do you think we should do today?" a smiling Celeste said, as she also stretched her arms toward the ceiling.

"I'm going to start by going for a run," Jack said. "I have spent the last week making phone calls, attending meetings and doing paperwork. I've been a total, lazy slug."

"Okay, you go for a run, I'll make a quick trip to the market to pick up some things and we'll meet back here and have a great breakfast."

"I like the way you think," Jack said as he headed for the bathroom. A couple of minutes later he came out wearing his running clothes. "I'll probably be close to an hour, I feel like a long run."

"See you later," she said as he went out the front door.

Angelina hadn't been waiting long when she saw Jack open the front door of the apartment. She watched through the open door as Celeste gave Jack a quick peck on the cheek. He did a few quick stretches on the stoop and started walking across the parking lot towards her. Angelina flipped her hood up and slipped out of the car. She headed directly for Jack, keeping her head down as she walked silently past him. He never gave her a second look as he started to focus on his run. He had no idea who she was, probably just another tenant from the apartment complex. He'd never bothered to get to know any of the neighbors; he just wasn't a "get to know you" kind of guy.

About 10 steps past Jack, Angelina slipped the gun out of the hoodie pocket and turned. She didn't say a word as she took aim at his back with both hands and pulled the trigger. Jack felt the hot sting just below his right shoulder blade as the bullet plowed through his body and exited between two ribs. He immediately knew he had been shot, it had happened before. *Kingsbury*, he thought as he tried to spin and get his unresponsive right hand up to his own weapon tucked in the shoulder holster under his left arm. The second shot hit him in the back near the upper left side, shattering his collar bone as it exited out the front near the top of his shoulder. No longer able to stand, he dropped to his knees and turned his head to try and look over his left shoulder. He was dizzy and the pain was unbearable. He could see the shooter in the hoodie now, advancing toward him. His eyes were bleary and unable to focus. He fell forward as he passed out from the pain.

Celeste had just come out of the apartment on her way to the market when she heard the first shot. She quickly turned away from the door and looked in the direction of the gun fire. She saw a small figure in a black hoodie standing over Jack, as he lay flat on the pavement. The person in the hoodie had a gun pointed at the back of his head. She instinctively reached into her purse, pulled the Glock 26 free, flipped the safety off and fired at the black hoodie.

Angelina had moved quickly, she wanted to finish the job and get out. She needed to be sure Jack didn't get up. She stood over his still, prone frame. Her gun pointed at the back of his head. Celeste's first shot was totally wild and shattered the windshield of a nearby car. She knew Jack was badly hurt and panic had taken over. Jack had been right, shooting at real people was way different than paper targets at a shooting range. Celeste's wild shot caught Angelina off guard. She instinctively turned to see where the shot had come from. Celeste took a deep breath, assumed a proper shooting stance like she had practiced so many times and fired two rapid shots at Angelina. Each shot found its way to the target. Two for two, *Jack would be proud*, she thought. Angelina staggered backward and began to fall. As she fell, she was able to raise her weapon, point it at Celeste, and pull the trigger one last time before she collapsed onto the pavement.

The human heart, in the grand scheme of things, is really no bigger than a small fist. Hitting it directly is rarely done even by the most highly skilled shooter with sophisticated weaponry and sighting equipment. Like the blind squirrel that finds a nut once in a while though, one in a million shots to the body finds its way to the heart. Such was Angelina's shot that day.

The nine millimeter bullet fired by Angelina as she fell backward hit Celeste just at the top of her left breast and tore directly through her heart. Celeste never felt any pain and was dead before her knees hit the sidewalk. One second she was firing to save Jack's life, an instant later she was gone.

At the sound of the first shot, several apartment tenants called 911. The first police car arrived less than five minutes later, followed by an ambulance. The second black and white arrived one minute later. Both officers had responded to a shots fired call, and neither knew what they were driving into. Each officer got out with weapons drawn and crouched cautiously behind the doors of their vehicles, carefully surveying the scene. Satisfied there was no imminent threat they cleared the ambulance attendants for entry. *Two females dead and one male unconscious with multiple gunshot wounds*, was the report radioed to dispatch. The EMT's wasted no time. They loaded Jack onto the gurney and into the ambulance in less than two minutes. One officer began the task of securing the scene with crime scene tape while the other began taking witness statements.

Chapter 49

The ambulance screamed through traffic racing for the emergency room at St. Joseph Medical Center. It was the closest hospital equipped for critical acute care. The ambulance driver radioed ahead with Jack's vital signs while the other EMT started an IV drip. Jack's vitals weren't good, there had been significant loss of blood and his blood pressure was dropping rapidly. The second shot had clipped a main artery and there was severe internal bleeding. The ER doc took one quick look at Jack and sent him straight to surgery. Several hours later Jack was put in an intensive care room with a fifty-fifty chance of survival.

He was in and out of consciousness for the next week and a half. At one point he looked over and saw Celeste sitting in a bedside chair smiling at him. Jack tried to speak but couldn't. He wondered why she wasn't talking to him. There was something strange about the way she looked, but Jack couldn't quite figure it out. It was like he was looking at her through a sheet of gauze. A few seconds later she faded away and so did he. It was that way for over a week. Jack would open his eyes and everything was fuzzy. An infection had developed in one of the wounds. He was delirious most of the time.

Another week went by and Jack finally woke without the fuzziness. The infection had finally been beaten back. He looked at the bedside chair. A solemn Alan Blackwell was sitting there. He smiled when he saw Jack's eyes open and not close again.

"Hello stranger," he said. "Welcome back to the land of the living."

"What happened," Jack managed to ask, as his eyes closed again to shut out the brightness of the room.

"Your old pal Garrison's wife did her very best to put you six feet under. What do you remember?"

"Not much, the last thing I remember was that I was going for a run. Everything has been so fuzzy and cloudy every time I've opened my eyes. Where's Celeste?"

"As near as we can tell, based on witness accounts, here's what happened. You were about to go for a run. Angelina Shepherd shot you twice, right after she passed you in the parking lot of the apartment complex. You took two in the back, both through and through. One did a lot of serious damage. We think she had been in a car, waiting for the right opportunity." Blackwell took a deep breath, leaned closer to the bed and put his hand on Jack's arm. "Celeste had just come out of the apartment when the shooting started. You were down and Angelina walked over and was about to put one in the back of your head when Celeste fired three times. The first one hit a car windshield, and then she hit Angelina with two quick ones. Celeste saved your life Jack.

She was a remarkable woman." *Was?* Jack was trying hard to focus. *Why did he say was?* "As Angelina fell she was able to return Celeste's fire," Blackwell continued. The CIA boss took another even deeper breath, searching for the right words. Jack could hear the stress in Blackwell's voice as the man struggled to continue. "Jack, Angelina's last shot as she was going down was one of those wild, crazy, one in a million shots. The bullet went straight through Celeste's heart. She died instantly, never knew what hit her. I'm so sorry."

Jack's eyes narrowed, he bit his quivering lower lip, took a deep breath and turned his head into the pillow, fighting back tears. His true feelings for Celeste, which he had never faced up to, were suddenly crystal clear to him. He loved her, and he'd never told her so.

"I'll leave you alone now Jack. Call me if you need anything, anything at all." Blackwell stood, took a piece of paper out of his picket and laid it on the bed next to Jack, and walked silently towards the door. He turned and looked back at Jack as he reached the door. There were no words that could offer his friend any comfort.

Tears ran down Jack's face as he slowly looked around the room. There were flowers and get well cards neatly arranged on every surface. All from Celeste's friends wishing a speedy recovery. He picked up the piece of paper left by Blackwell. It was Celeste's obituary from the Houston Chronicle. The funeral service had been a week earlier. Attached to the obit was a newspaper article about the shooting. The article explained how Celeste had saved his life as he laid on the pavement in the parking lot. The article went on to explain that ballistic tests run on the bullets fired by the deranged woman's gun were a match to those that had killed her husband, Garrison Shepherd only a few months earlier. No mention was made of Jack or his relationship to Celeste.

Chapter 50

A little over a month later, still dazed and hurting from his loss Jack had left the hospital and was on a flight to Vienna. He was going to tell Inez and her kids why Trini had been killed. He never caught Trini's killer, but vowed someday he would.

He was on his third drink as he looked out the window at the Atlantic 25,000 feet below. He wanted to be asleep. He wanted to awaken and find it had all been a horrible dream. But he couldn't sleep and even if he could, it wouldn't have been a dream. It had all happened. He held up his empty glass to the flight attendant as she walked by.

"One more please," he said. The pocket full of pills he was still taking eased the pain in his body. He was using the alcohol to try and ease the pain in his mind. It wasn't working.

He had set out to find a sniper who'd killed an OPEC analyst. Why couldn't that have been all there was to it? He hadn't found the killer, but he had found who was behind it; one bad guy down and behind bars. That should've been the end of it, but it wasn't. His best friend had been murdered and his killer brought to justice, but at what cost? A cost far too high and far too hard to live with. The only woman he ever truly loved was gone and he was to blame. If only he hadn't been so obsessed with finding Garrison's killer. If only he hadn't pressed Angelina so hard. It would just have been a matter of time before she would have been caught. Celeste would still be alive.

Jack thought of the sailboats he had seen on the Potomac River and his vision of being at the helm of one with Celeste at his side. He pressed his head against the cool hard window and wished it all would go away. He needed it all to go away.

Several hundred miles away, Ballinger sat on the balcony of his Paris apartment, sipping a glass of Glenlivet and enjoying the still, evening air. His gaze wandered to the street below where two young lovers were out for an evening stroll. Ah, the romance of Paris. He was glad to be, temporarily at least, out of a job. He was no longer concerned about Kingsbury, his plan had worked perfectly. The good Senator was going away for a long, long time.

He took a sip of his premium Scotch and answered his ringing cell phone. It was Bastrop calling from Brussels. "Speak," Ballinger said.

"I hear Santiago Chile is great this time of year. I have another job for you," said the voice on the other end of the call.

Acknowledgements

Writing a book is no easy task and there are always more people involved than just the author. I owe a huge debt of gratitude to the following people: Aven Wright-McIntosh for her amazing editing skills and suggestions. Tom Fauria for the great idea about glissading, glad you weren't impaled on your roll down the mountain. Police Officer S.R. Trotter for the great ride along and insights into a police officer's mind. Rex Barrong for his expertise on a variety of law enforcement matters. My wife Pat for her editing and suggestions all along the way. And Marta Durfee for her read through and tweaking the final draft.

.

18921827R00173

Made in the USA
San Bernardino, CA
04 February 2015